Advance Praise

"Wisniewski: a riotously original voice."
  —Jonathan Lethem

"Mark Wisniewski's prose is incisive and crisp, bracing and in the best sense destructive, like a straight shot of excellent gin. Part Carson McCullers, part Truman Capote, part Elmore Leonard, *Show Up, Look Good* is ultimately a highly original, entertaining, and disturbing read, accurate but precisely off-center. Just when you think you know how it moves, it proves you wrong, and you're delighted. Wisniewski is that crafty a craftsman, that intelligent a writer."
  —T. R. Hummer, author of *Walt Whitman in Hell*

"Forget *My Sister Eileen*. With wit and insight, Wisniewski shows what really happens when a resourceful, optimistic, upbeat young woman from the Midwest comes to Manhattan to make it."
  —Molly Giles, author of *Rough Translations*, winner of the Flannery O'Connor
    Award for Short Fiction

"With equal parts rue and satire, Mark Wisniewski's thirty-four-year-old Midwestern heroine, Michelle, flees love gone wrong at home to start over with nerve and independence in Manhattan. Her picaresque misadventures and her encounters with characters odd, pretentious, and menacing prove as haunting as Holden Caulfield's."
  —DeWitt Henry, author of *Sweet Dreams*, founding editor of *Ploughshares*

"*Show Up, Look Good* is a rare, gleaming gem: as soon as I turned the final page, I felt bereft because I didn't want it to end. Wisniewski has a poet's heart, a jester's wit, and a comedian's dead-on timing. This is a novel to savor."
  —Christine Sneed, author of *Portraits of a Few People I've Made Cry*, winner of
    The Grace Paley Prize in Short Fiction

"This novel about a thirty-something woman who travels from Kankakee, Illinois, to New York to 'make it' deepens in unexpected and moving ways. Wisniewski ventriloquizes with perfect pitch his female narrator, who has a real talent for getting into trouble. *Show Up, Look Good* is funny, dark, poignant, and unsettling."
　—Kelly Cherry, author of *We Can Still Be Friends*

"*Show Up, Look Good* is a rollicking, laugh-out-loud romp of a novel, a picaresque spin through fin-de-siècle New York as seen through the eyes of its intrepid, Midwestern-born heroine. Love, loneliness, roommates from hell, hipsters, the mob, and murder all play starring roles in this delightful book, and Wisniewski does justice to them all."
　—Ben Fountain, author of *Brief Encounters with Che Guevara*

"In *Show Up, Look Good* Mark Wisniewski demonstrates again why he is one of the most versatile, entertaining, and accomplished writers of his generation."
　—Richard Burgin, author of *Rivers Last Longer* and *The Identity Club: New and Selected Stories* and Editor, *Boulevard*

"There's good writing, and then there's kick-ass writing, and Mark Wisniewski's storytelling is absolutely kick-ass. I wanted to jump up and down."
　—Katherine Center, author of *Everyone Is Beautiful* and *Bright Side of Disaster*

"*Show Up, Look Good* made me laugh out loud at both Wisniewski's sharp wit and the narrator's propensity for making the mess of her life messier. It's a page-turner, a thrill, and a dark love song to New York City. What a terrific novel."
　—Diana Spechler, author of *Who By Fire* and *Skinny*

"You're a slave to Manhattan even if the cost of living drives you out to Queens. Incongruities like that, nutty and yet right-on, delight us in every scene of Mark Wisniewski's *Show Up, Look Good*. A witty and original take on New York swing, this novel can both analyze an urban tribe as smartly as Richard Price and threaten murder with the offhand aplomb of Jonathan Lethem. The fresh face in the urban canyons has rarely glowed with such laughter and astonishment, even as it earns the bloody smears of a warrior."
　— John Domini, author of *A Tomb on the Periphery*

Show Up, Look Good

a novel

Mark Wisniewski

Gival Press

Arlington, Virginia

Published by Gival Press, an imprint of Gival Press, LLC.

For information please write:
Gival Press, LLC
P. O. Box 3812
Arlington, VA 22203
www.givalpress.com

First edition

ISBN: 978-1-92-8589-60-0
eISBN: 978-1-92-8589-66-2
Library of Congress Control Number: 2011925414

Cover Artwork by Andrew Barthelmes.
Design by Ken Schellenberg.

Acknowledgments

Portions of this book have appeared in the following: *New England Review, Boulevard, The 1999 Pushcart Prize XXIII: Best of the Small Presses, Green Hills Literary Lantern, Cimarron Review, Oasis, The Vincent Brothers Review,* and *Crossconnect*. Grateful acknowledgment is made to all editors and staff of those publications, as well as to Clarence Major, Caroline Langston, Jack Smith, and Richard Burgin, for their Pushcart nominations of material herein, and to former *Ploughshares* editor DeWitt Henry, whose attention and encouragement regarding an unconventional short story led me to envision this novel, and to Robert Giron and Ken Schellenberg, for their talents and dedication to the design, production, and publication of this book. Gratitude indeed to Tim Malloy, John Mino and the inimitable Eric Osserman, for all their storytelling in the Georgetown days.

Unending thanks to Elizabeth.

Chapter 1

I know of a secret murder, and I've loved a speechless man, and sometimes I'd like to tell someone about how death and love have changed my life, but any of three thoughts give me pause. For one, if I talk about the murder, I myself could be killed. I can't know how true this is, but the speechless man said it was, and even though he's disappointed me, I trust him. Two, if someone's murdered, she's murdered, and talking about her will never change that. Then there's the reality very few people care to face: unless you have majestic beauty or power, your secrets rarely matter to anyone but yourself.

Especially if you think too much. Which, apparently, is a problem of mine— at least if you ask Thom, my one-and-only ex-fiancé. How he came to inform me of this is something I imagine he's kept as a secret of his own, because it involves what one might call his sexual preference.

I found out about this preference after we'd dated for eleven years: we'd been that college couple who spends every minute together, with everyone else laughing at them behind their backs. During those eleven years, we made it through a pregnancy scare, his mother's nervous breakdown, and the Macarena craze by drinking quasi-moderately and watching *Apocalypse Now* at least three dozen times. Finally we set a wedding date, but then we stopped having sex, and we decided we were both way out of shape and joined a health club and lost weight, though I lost mine because I'd begun smoking cigarettes behind his back. All of this might seem like a fairly representative courtship of two burgeoning adults in Kankakee, Illinois, where we were born and raised, but then I woke one night and he wasn't beside me, and I saw light beneath our bedroom door and worried he was sick, so I opened the door and found him on my couch with his boxer shorts down past his knees, having his way with, well, a marital aid.

And I'd rather not dwell on the specifics of that particular item, but I will say it had been designed to substitute for the primary female sex organ, which felt so degrading of both me and him, all I could say was, "Thom?"

"Yeah," he said.

"Where did we...get that?"

"North Carolina," he said.

"You sent for it?"

His eyes moved from mine to the TV, which was off. He still had the thing around his thing. "I ordered it," he said. "On the internet."

Part of me, right then, wanted to tell him to leave the apartment and never come back. The other part told me to be careful— because maybe this was one of those touch-and-go moments when someone you love needs to be held.

"You don't think it's a little...unnecessary?" I asked. "I mean, you already sort of have one of those."

"You mean yours?"

"Correct."

He faked a cough. "I wanted to try something new."

"Those aren't exactly the words I wanted to hear."

"Did you want me to lie?"

"No."

"Actually," he said, "if you want me to be really honest, I wanted to try something that didn't involve so much thought."

Now virtually all of me wanted to tell him to leave. "What do you mean, 'so much thought'?" I asked. I made eye contact now: I wasn't going to let a plastic vagina have the upper hand.

"Do you really want to get into this?" he asked.

"Why wouldn't I?"

He disengaged himself from the two plastic lips, pulled up his boxers, and sighed. "It comes down to this," he said. "You think too much."

"Oh, do I?" I said.

"It's like, when we, you know, make love, I know you're thinking all kinds of thoughts, and, well, when I know that's the case, it kind of...ruins it for me."

"Thom," I said. "I already stopped *talking* while we do it— because you didn't like *that*. And if I did talk while we do it, which would, by the way, make it better for me, I probably wouldn't think as much as I do. I mean, I'm trying to work with you here, but when it comes right down to it, I'd say you can't have it both ways."

"What are you saying? You want me to leave?"

"I think so," I said.

Which I didn't mean entirely. But he walked into the bedroom, put on clothes, wiped his keys and change and wallet off the top of his dresser, and left. I thought, for the rest of that night and the next day or two, that he'd left merely because he'd been embarrassed by his obvious excitement over (read: inside) his friend the sex toy, and that he'd return any time, but he never came back. He did call me two months later, but by then I'd heard from mutual friends that he was dating a six-pack-ab blond, so I played that conversation with him *very* non-chalantly, sticking mostly to questions about his job as a tree surgeon, and after that, neither of us ever called the other, and then, in the middle of a night when I couldn't sleep but had no one except myself to blame, I knew I had to leave town.

So I drove from Kankakee to New York, stewing pretty much the whole way about how, in the mind of a man I'd once thought the world of, I thought far too much. I joined morning rush hour traffic over the George Washington Bridge as though Manhattan-born-and-raised, then parked in a spot on Ninth Avenue that opened as if for me personally. I walked until I found myself in Soho numbed by a kind of relieved confusion, checked out a *Voice* classifieds section, called at least a dozen numbers about subleases without reaching a human being, then finally spoke with an old woman named Etta who wanted someone to do chores in exchange for a break on rent—only five hundred a month for a room in her place as long as you walked her Shih Tzu and shopped for her groceries—and even though five hundred eclipsed the rent I'd paid for a two-bedroom in Kankakee, I was so excited about the prospects of getting a room without needing to sleep in some *hostel*, I told her I'd take it.

"Not so fast," she said. She had a Norwegian accent, and Norwegian accents intimidated me. "We should meet first, no?" she asked.

No, I wanted to say, because to me, it didn't matter how she looked or what kind of chemistry I felt around her. After all, we were talking about a jump from a cinder block apartment building in Illinois to an actual Manhattan address. Then she gave me the address itself, explaining that it was just off Eighth Avenue on 49th, and I said I'd be there pronto, then took a cab feeling lucky about where we'd stop if we weren't broadsided first.

Etta's building wasn't a high-rise though I wasn't there to quibble, and she had no apparent health problems and didn't seem shocked by my appearance despite my lack of a shower in thirty-eight hours. Her apartment smelled of eucalyptus and had ceilings that were some two feet higher than I'd imagined, her living room more hip than geriatric. In her kitchen, on an antique farm table, she'd laid out blue and white china, ornate but unpolished silverware, pumpernickel bagels cut in thirds, and nickel-thin slices of liverwurst, and as we sat on opposite sides of the table, she told me to help myself. I actually love liverwurst, but I didn't want to blow her impression of me by leaving a pinkish smear on a corner of my mouth, so I took two bagel chunks (stabbing them gently with a fork, as she had), thanked her for them, and braced myself for dozens of prying questions, but essentially all she did was tell stories about when she'd been young: how she'd traveled to Belgium and got lost for twelve hours; how her father had manufactured doilies that had been used by some prince; how she'd loved her pet rabbit but it ran away through the front door when her cousins were visiting—and she hadn't had a pet since, until she'd bought her Shih Tzu, whose name was Tino, and who was, she mentioned, outside in the tiny yard behind the building. She did ask about my parents, and I told her my mother had died just after I'd been born, and she said "Terrible" in a way that conveyed empathy but allowed our conversation to stay cool, which is how I still prefer people to be about my mother—and death in general.

Then she showed me what would be my room. It could have been bigger but had the same high ceiling and a huge window overlooking 49th. She mentioned that I couldn't "entertain male guests," watching my face as she did, though if I weren't quite happy about that rule, there was no way I let it show. Then it hit me that she was talking about the apartment as if it were ours, and I told myself I was a bona fide resident of the city, but she walked me to the bathroom and said, "I'm needing you to know that the most important thing in the world to me is personal hygiene."

"Me, too," I said, as if I'd exfoliated an hour earlier.

"I absolutely must bathe every night before bed."

"That's fine with me. I'll just shower in the morning."

"And I'm needing you to feel comfortable when you help me," she said, "because the last woman who lived here either didn't care about proper cleansing or was simply too shy."

Her word choice here, I have to admit, threw me. "What do you mean 'help' you?" I asked.

"Bathe."

"Oh."

"You find that problematic?"

"No. I just didn't know that was part of the deal."

"I mentioned it on the phone, no?" she said, which put me in a spot since she *hadn't* mentioned it, and if there's one thing I'd change if I ruled the world, it's when people claim to have said things they actually haven't said. But the bathroom had an adorable pedestal sink, and we were in Manhattan, and, the way I saw it, I was one correct answer away from having found a place to live in Midtown, which, from what I'd read, was impossible.

"I guess you did mention it," I said.

"I'm wanting to have you help me bathe right now." She pulled aside the shower curtain and opened the tub faucet. "So we'll both know what to expect."

"Sure," I said, and that word tripped off a chain of events that were not at all in line with that plan you have in the back of your head about how your day might unravel. For starters, she disrobed immediately, which was slightly off-putting. I'm not a prude, but think about it: one minute we're strangers, and two bagel chunks later, I see her pubic hair—all because a tree surgeon penetrated a portable vagina delivered by third class mail. Then, after she got in the tub, she directed me to follow her entire "hygienic sequence," which required me to wash all of her, beginning with the skin around her eyes and getting more private until I'd attended to what most people would rather call her privates and leave at that. Worse, she wanted me to be, as she put it, "thorough" (pronounced without either "h"). And: after I washed her, she had me stand beside the tub while she rested in the suds and got *sleepy*, and her head eased down the porcelain and began slipping beneath the water, so I leaned over the tub and tried to hold her up by the shoulders while saying "Etta?" loudly enough to wake her yet softly enough not to sound peeved. And I'm not exactly big—four-eleven-and-a quarter in sneakers with new soles—and she wasn't what you'd call a little old lady. Her arms and legs were thin, but she was gangly as well as slippery, so as I struggled to hold her up, I brimmed with panic. You know: What if she'd *drown*? And she did wake up, but the question was whether I wanted to be responsible for someone's life every night just to be able to conduct mine in Manhattan, which became an immediate conundrum when, after she'd had me dry her and help her into a fresh outfit, she asked, "Well, my little Michelle, are we roommates?"

"Can I think about it?" I asked.

"Have you other possibilities?"

"Yes," I said, and I really hate to lie, because once you do, how can you expect honesty from anyone?

"Then maybe you should take one of them," she said. "As I mentioned, the last girl was shy, and that was a definite problem."

"But I think I want to live here."

"You *think* so. I want someone who *knows*."

"I just wanted to check...around. So I could know for sure."

"Then you go. And check. And we'll both think until we both know."

You blew it, I thought. "So I can come back and—"

"We'll see, Michelle. Others have called. You go and look."

And I'll never be sure, but, for a moment, there might have been the slightest bit of insecurity in her voice. What I do know is that, as she led me past the liverwurst on our way toward the door, I felt insanely hungry, and that, after I'd said goodbye and she hadn't, I squared myself with the possibility that, Thom's opinion aside, I *did* think too much. Or at least that I couldn't have been more of a fool than to drive all the way to New York, have a chance at living there fall into my hands, and lose it by being inflexible.

Then I was out of her building, walking toward Eighth Avenue, which was far more busy than it had been when the cab had dropped me off, as if the congested traffic were telling me that the only metropolitan area where I could fit was Kankakee, Illinois. Or maybe, I told myself, it's telling you to press on, and I wandered up Broadway to the Ed Sullivan Theater, where David Letterman's blue and yellow marquis reminded me that I liked to laugh. I stared at that marquis as tourists bumped my shoulders, and then I realized I was grinning—because Etta's neighborhood all at once felt like the center of a carefree world.

I ran back to her building and pressed her buzzer repeatedly until she let me up. And it took some vigorous begging, as well as cooing over Tino and allowing him to lick my upper lip despite his bad breath, but, finally, she agreed to our deal. And yes, I'd committed myself to a nightly bathing session with a woman I hardly knew, but she was old enough to be my grandmother, and I'd be bathing her in Manhattan, the only place where, as I saw things then, untold numbers of people and I could live with our thoughts forever.

Chapter 2

It didn't take long to find out that, despite Etta's having bristled when I'd hesitated to room with her, she was as nice as anyone gets. Even when she was tired she was never cross, and she had an aura about her you rarely feel around people, a benevolence that seemed to glow from her. I wouldn't call her a saint, because she could cuss like a pieceworker, but I never got the impression she was like most decent people, who, behind their kindness, seem to want something in return. Her Shih Tzu Tino was so well-adjusted and sweet, you just knew her goodness had rubbed off on him: he lived to be held. And when I shopped for her, her grocery list always included seven slices of American cheese, which she'd give him only because he loved it—not because he'd done some damned trick. And even though she watched her money down to the penny, her list always ended with the words, "three dollar snack for Michelle."

My only worry, after she and I squared away things such as which shelves of the fridge I could use, involved my own finances, because Thom had maxed and defaulted on every credit card I could get in Kankakee, and all I had in my Kankakee Federal checking account was eight dollars and change. This account, though, was attached to a savings account my mother had set up for me shortly before she died, and I'd always left that money alone because she'd supposedly wanted me to use it for my honeymoon, not to mention her death had made it feel sacred. But now that Thom and I had parted as we had, a honeymoon seemed preposterous, and being in Manhattan made me feel as if I'd reached a sacred point in my life, so those savings now seemed usable. They were enough to make my initial payment to Etta (first and last month's rent—she let me slide on a se-curity deposit) and leave me with enough for my second month's rent and maybe enough groceries until I found work.

As far as work went, I didn't want to wait tables because, from what I'd heard, *everyone* who moves to Manhattan hopes they'll amount to something, then waits tables. It also didn't help that, just before I left Kankakee, I'd been fired from my job as a bank teller for allegedly stealing. What happened was an old man took advantage of me in one of those change-making scams, which I might not have fallen for had I not been disadvantaged by exhaustion from a late night with my friends (during which I heard yet again about Thom's girlfriend) and the fact that this con artist was dressed as a priest, with the white collar *and* a black cardigan.

My point is, I'd been fired for the presumed commission of The Cardinal Sin of the Banking Industry—dipping into the till—so my "career" as a teller was over, and I was determined not to wait tables, but of course I needed cash. Living in Midtown, though, amidst all that flaunted wealth you see wherever you walk, I felt hopeful. I figured that if I thought, as those dot-com geeks used to say, outside the box, I could come up with respectable employment. I mean, whenever you see one of those documentaries on the making of a film, there's always a production assistant who's in her early twenties at most, and you just know she got her job because, more than anything, she had the spine to refuse to wait tables.

As it turned out, the gig I wound up with was related to show business, but I was no assistant—I was my own boss. And I lucked into it by coming up with an idea almost a week after I'd moved in with Etta, while I was bathing her. I can't say why the idea hit me then, other than that, when I'd wash her, I'd think of something other than what I was doing, since bathing her often lent itself to our unspoken agreement to distract ourselves. When I'd shampoo her, for example, she'd sing zany Norwegian songs, or tell me this story about two elderly people whose spouses died, about how they, the two survivors, mourned for a few years, then searched everywhere for each other and met on the internet, then arranged to meet again in person (when they were eighty-two) in the same park where they'd "wooed" each other as teens, and they fell in love all over again, married each other, and experienced the best sex of their lives. And they felt this happiness—but, *damn* me, my thoughts are taking me away from how I came up with my idea about how to earn cash.

It was while I was rinsing her left armpit that the idea struck: to make my rent, I'd sell Letterman tickets on Broadway. Two nights earlier, I'd been watching Dave in my room with the sound low for Etta's sake, and he'd joked about how his show was the hottest ticket on Broadway. When he said that I laughed, but then, the next night, while I was watching him, I remembered that I'd gotten two free tickets for his show a week before I left Kankakee, after sending out for them a month earlier. And I thought: No doubt I forgot to bring them. Still, I checked the pockets of the laundry I'd scooped off my floor before I left Kankakee (wherever I've lived, there's always been a foot of clothes on my floor—I am, I'll admit, a terminal slob) and there, in a back pocket of a pair of jeans I didn't like any more, was the *Late Show* envelope, with tickets inside for the following Thursday. Bingo, I thought. I'm going to see Dave. But the *next* night, while rinsing the previously mentioned armpit, the thought of *two* tickets made me wish I could go with a date, and I considered taking Etta, but she and I still didn't know each other well enough to relax together into pure fun, so that wouldn't have worked. Then I remembered how Dave and Paul Shaffer had mentioned movie stars they'd soon feature as guests, and it hit me that maybe Dave's show was indeed the hottest ticket on Broadway—and I could sell the pair I had for at least some of the next month's rent.

So I tried. And it was easy. I simply woke on the morning of the show and strolled over to the Ed Sullivan Theater, where at least fifty people were waiting in line for stand-by tickets (which work only if people with mailed-for tickets don't fill the studio), and told the hapless souls at the end of the line that I could guarantee two of them could see that evening's show—and a crowd grew around me. I'd thought $50 apiece would have been great, but a guy with obvious hair plugs offered $150 for the pair, and two college kids offered me a hundred apiece, and bids from there sent me home with $350 in my pocket: cash, no taxes, no questions asked.

The feeling I had when I returned to my room was something I'll never forget: on one hand, I wouldn't see Dave myself, but on the other, I'd never earned so much so easily—it took three minutes to make the sale, which, if my math is correct, came to something like $6,000 an hour. So I hit the post office and bought fifty of those postcards with postage already on them, and sent ten requests to the Ed Sullivan Theater for myself care of Etta, as well as requests for my father and aunts and several oddball cousins who now might as well have been strangers—and everyone I knew who didn't care much about Dave—then phoned them to say I'd moved, going on to mention I'd requested tickets for them, knowing they'd never fly to see a show they rarely watched, telling them that, if they didn't want the tickets, they could send them to me so I could see Dave.

I did lose faith after a month passed and no one's tickets had arrived. At least mine hadn't; I had to assume no one else's did either, since if I'd call them and ask if their tickets arrived, they might think I was using them. I didn't think I was using them, because had they asked me to do the same for them, I would have said yes, but in any case it was becoming clear that the same demand that made Dave's tickets worth cash had increased the number of requests and caused a delay that had me in a bind.

Stress, of course, escalated. If nothing else, I needed to sell my car, a maroon Plymouth Reliant. This disturbed me because I'd bought that car just after college, when I was sure Thom and I would marry and have jobs that paid enough for a house and kids and the pointless big ticket items Thom wanted, like a bass boat in our driveway and a hot tub in a deck. Plus: it was *The Reliant*. I mean, that's what Thom and I had called it. And its reliability had always lived up to its name, even after Thom put antifreeze where you're supposed to put oil. Over the years it might have proved more reliable than Thom and I had been to each other, and maybe something in us had always known that, so it's possible we'd loved it more than we'd loved each other. And I know it's hokey to refer to your car as "The" anything, but that's what Thom and I had done, and the realization that something you and your lover once did sounds hokey doesn't mean you forget about it when that lover has left your life.

All of this to say that, now that it was time for The Reliant to go, I fell into sentimentality. Then I fought sentiment because rent was coming due and a question needed an answer: How do you sell a used car in Manhattan? You can walk the city for days, I realized, and never see a used car lot. And when I looked in classified ads, even in those (tabloid-sized) used-car-person's kinds of papers, there were very few listings for used cars, which suggested New York papers charged more for an ad than you could make selling anything except maybe an almost new Mercedes. And Etta told me about a business that sold people's cars for them, but a woman I called there offered an insultingly low sixty dollars for The Reliant, albeit with a British accent.

My solution: put a sign in the car itself. Which should have worked because I parked the damned thing in a different spot every morning. Which sometimes took an entire morning. Because to acquire an affordable spot (that is, a free one), I had to deal with alternate-side parking, which meant I had to wake every morning and get to The Reliant before eight, to move it before it was booted, ticketed, and/or towed, then find an open spot immediately after eight on the opposite side of the street—or the legal side of another street—before anyone else beat me to it.

And *many* people played this game. You'd think most New Yorkers couldn't, owing to their need to work, but between 7:57 and 8:03, there are hundreds, possibly thousands, of saps in Manhattan trying, against rush hour traffic, to outsmart one-way streets and no-left-turn signs to stop in a place where their car can sit for a day—and to claim that place without driving for two and a half hours to find it.

Which actually happened to me. What also happened (more than once) was that I'd wake up just after eight—and grab my keys and run out of Etta's building in nothing but my robe and sneakers, then run down sidewalks to beat the omnipresent tow truck to my formerly precious spot. Once when that happened, I sprinted four blocks and reached the spot and a Volvo was there instead of The Reliant, and I thought, Great. They towed it. But then a man in *his* robe ran up to the Volvo and got in and drove off, and I realized I was standing beside the spot I'd used two days earlier, not the day before, which meant The Reliant was someplace else. And when I'm in a snit and just waking up, memory isn't my strongest point, so I jogged around Midtown holding closed the throat of my robe, up and down most of the Fifties between Eighth and Tenth Avenues, wishing I could just light a cigarette and walk, until, on 56th off of Ninth, I saw it, The Reliant, waiting for me like a miracle.

I was so happy right then, I actually cried. Lest I *think* too much, though, I should return to the point at hand: with The Reliant making it around from spot to spot like that every day, I figured a sign in the window should help me sell it easily. "FOR SALE, $1,500, 212-555-2439" was what I stuck inside the rear window with duct tape Etta's super had left in the kitchen.

But after four days, not a single person called. Except for a guy who woke Etta and me at 3:17 AM to say he'd seen me get in my car the previous morning, and did I need a little company before dawn?

"Absolutely not," I told him, though that wasn't exactly the truth.

Chapter 3

With rent due in six days, I brought the price down to a thousand. This irked me because, given what I now paid for necessities such as whole wheat bread and hair product, The Reliant and I deserved twice that. But still there were no calls, not even from Mr. Sexually Frustrated. Then, with four days left before rent was due and three prices crossed out and "BEST OFFER" neatly and passive-aggressively printed on a new sign, the phone rang, and Etta said it was for me, but it was a friend of mine named Barb, who announced her forthcoming visit from Kankakee because she'd found a last-minute bargain on a flight to Newark—and she was in O'Hare and on her way.

What do you say to someone so presumptuous? Do you mention that Newark might as well be a suburb of Philadelphia? I didn't tell her this, and for various reasons, one of which was that years earlier, after she and Thom had themselves a three-week flirtation festival, I slept with her boyfriend. And I mean slept, because that's essentially all this guy and I did. Not that sex hadn't been possible. It was just that, when he asked if I wanted to, as he put it, "have intercourse," I said, "I'm not sure." What I wanted right then was to talk about what was on our minds, which I suppose proves that, yes, I'm more into people's thoughts than what they can prove with their bodies, but anyway he didn't say a thing for the rest of the night, just spooned me like the loser I now consider him.

After that half-baked tryst, though, Barb and Thom suspected us of having engaged in some grand, erotic feast, and Barb herself finally learned we merely spooned from Thom, after I admitted the spooning to him, and from then on Barb displayed a superiority complex (obviously based on insecurity) when-ever she was around both me and her boyfriend, whose name, by the way, was Dwayne.

Naturally, I couldn't fathom why she wanted to visit me now. Her take on the spooning seemed to be that it meant a threat by me: Look what I didn't do but *could* do if you ever cross me. Still, a cheerful Barb showed up at Etta's building after a bus ride from Newark to Midtown that lasted longer than her flight, and she wanted to drink, and I found us a place with a cowboy theme on the Upper West Side, where I couldn't tell if her indulgence in beer was to avoid thoughts about the spooning or to make the spooning easier to discuss. And I certainly didn't know that, after she shrieked at a bartender about his having made a pass at her, being bounced from the bar was the last thing I'd remember until the phone rang at seven the next morning, a woman telling me her brother saw the sign in The Reliant—and wanted to buy.

"Can your brother," I asked this woman, "pay in cash?"

"Yes," she said. "He can bring cash now. We can be at the car in half an hour."

The crucial question required false offhandedness: "Where did your brother see the car, ma'am?"

"On 76th Street. West of Columbus."

"I'll be there in twenty minutes," I said, and I hung up.

"Be where?" Barb asked from under Etta's spare comforter on the floor.

"The Reliant," I said. "I have to sell it."

"Today?"

"Yes."

"Why?"

"I don't have time to explain."

I got out of bed and shuffled to the mirror Etta called my vanity. I didn't want to deal with Barb that day—or with anticipation of an argument over my submission to Dwayne's spooning. I checked my eyes for puffiness (a surprisingly non-puffy day), left the room, walked down the hall, knocked to see if Etta were in the bathroom, then locked myself inside. When I returned to my room, Barb had put on brown corduroys, a tangerine-colored blouse, and her infamous lavender bowling shoes. She stooped to double-knot her laces. "I'm going with you," she said.

"Then let's go," I said. I couldn't miss the woman's brother because I could no longer stand to obsess about parking spots—plus, of course, I needed rent. I grabbed my purse. "Hurry," I said, and Barb squirted ahead of me and led us outside.

Walking up Eighth Avenue, she and I were uncommonly silent. Then again, 7:30 AM has never been the ideal time of day for me to share friendship, strained or otherwise. After I grabbed Barb's wrist to have her follow my left onto 76th, three Asian people approached, a woman and two men, and the woman noticed me and waved, and then they were so close I felt that panic you feel when you're alone on an elevator with your boss.

In no-name blue jeans and a faded Old Navy T-shirt, the woman, like me, obviously hadn't taken her bite out of The Apple. "I'm here to interpret," she said, engaging Barb's eyes.

"And I'm here," I said, "to sell."

One of the men grinned. A chisel couldn't have handled the tartar between his incisors. "He's my brother," the woman said. The Money Man, I thought, and he nodded. "As is he," the woman said, and she pointed to the other man, who was circling The Reliant, studying its maroon paint.

"It's hardly scratched at all," I told him, but he continued circling. He pointed at the steering wheel and flicked his wrist, so I opened the driver's side door and cranked on the engine, and he put his ear against the hood and held it there. The Mechanic, I thought, and again he began circling The Reliant, his brother circling in the opposite direction, both of them inspecting, pointing at nicks, and whistling.

"This is weird," Barb said.

"I should've said you were a buyer," I whispered.

"Implying what? You and I aren't friends?"

"Relax, Barb," I said, though my hangover made me wonder if our friendship was worth what it took.

The woman and The Money Man conversed in Chinese. The Mechanic lit up a Salem, and the woman stepped in front of me and asked, "How much?"

"I can get twelve hundred from someone else next week," I said, obvious bull. "But I'll take a thousand because I need it for rent."

"Five hundred," The Money Man said.

"Hey," Barb said. "He wasn't supposed to speak English."

"He knows numbers," the woman explained, and The Money Man grinned, and his tartar worked as a bargaining tool: softened up by his apparent lack of a dental plan, I held up seven fingers. The Money Man held up five, yelled Chinese at the woman, then glanced at me and said, "Five." Then I realized he was making an offer without driving the car, so I dropped a finger, but just as I did, he turned to face The Mechanic. I dropped another finger and yelled, "Five!"

"Are you serious?" the woman asked.

"If five is okay with your brother," I said.

"It's okay," The Money Man said.

"Hey, that wasn't *numbers*," Barb said.

"You have it in cash, right?" I asked The Money Man.

Chinese whispers turned into three-way Chinese shouting. I double-checked the no-parking sign across the street, which told me that, in a matter of minutes, The Reliant would need to be moved yet again.

"She nodded," Barb told me.

"You nodded?" I asked the woman.

"I meant my brother has the cash," she explained.

"Then I'll make a contract," I said, and I found a pen in my purse, as well as a Tex-Mex take-out menu. Above the restaurant's name, I printed out our deal with as much legalese as I could muster, and then, below the name, I wrote it out again.

"I need more sleep," Barb said.

I tore the menu in half, signed each piece, then handed both—with my pen—to The Money Man. He raised an eyebrow at my handwriting and muttered something to the woman.

"Does your brother have a question?" I asked her.

"Parking tickets," she said as she glanced at Barb. "Does the car have any?"

"It will if he doesn't sign," I said. "In fact, that's why I'm selling it. I mean, I hate moving it every day. Which I do to *avoid* tickets."

The Money Man's elbow nudged the side of the woman's arm.

"Can you prove no tickets?" she asked me.

"Call the DMV," I said, and then Barb and I listened to more Chinese. And this time they really went at it.

"Call from where?" the woman finally asked me.

The Money Man handed me the contracts. "You haven't signed them," I said, and he shrugged and handed back the pen.

"He wants to call the DMV first," the woman said, and I wanted to put my foot down but hated to risk scaring them off.

"There are payphones on Columbus," I said. "Listen, I've got to move this car."

More Chinese erupted, this time less angrily. Barb sighed and folded her arms.

"You didn't have to come," I told her.

"You mean to Manhattan?" she asked.

"To sell The Reliant," I said. "Though just for the record, it was your idea to visit Manhattan."

"Do you have fifty cents?" the woman asked me.

"Does your brother have the five hundred?" Barb asked her.

"Quiet, Barb," I said. Searching my purse for change, I found a dime and two pennies. Then I did something I preferred not to do: ask Barb for thirty-eight of her precious cents.

She cleared her throat, thereby announcing that I was in for the I-have-more-cash-than-you-do aspect of her superiority, which had been a sticking point between us since we'd met. "I'll give him the fifty cents," she said, and she sighed. She checked a pocket of her brown corduroys and told me, "You get tonight's first round." Then she handed two quarters to The Money Man, who walked *away* from Columbus.

Barb and the woman stared at The Reliant. The woman kicked the left rear tire. "New," I said, and Barb nodded, and a police car turned from Columbus onto 76th, rolled toward us, and stopped.

"Move the vehicle, sir," the cop told The Mechanic. "The street sweeper is four blocks away."

"No English," The Mechanic said.

"That cop's a babe," Barb whispered into my ear.

"So have sex with him," I said, and I made eye contact with the cop and shouted, "We'll move it in a minute, sir."

He studied me, then The Reliant. Then he rolled off. The woman sighed. Barb said, "I *should* have had sex with him," and I wanted to ask, What would Dwayne think about that?

The Money Man returned and whispered into his sister's ear.

"Well?" I asked. "Do we have a deal?"

"Almost," the woman said.

"But there weren't any tickets," I said, "were there?"

"No," the woman said. "But he's worried about getting insurance."

"God," Barb muttered, and the woman knotted her eyebrows. "Maybe," Barb said, "the guy doesn't want your car."

And right then I felt this coddled transaction unravel. I glossed over my disappointment by picturing Barb and me cabbing off to drink later that night, and I realized drinking with her hadn't been fun for years.

"My brother wants the car," the woman said. "He just needs his insurance."

"Then have him call his insurance guy," I said.

"His insurance guy has no phone."

"Then I don't know," I said. "I'm trying to entertain a friend here." I folded the contracts and shoved them into a back pocket and walked off—the hell with all of them, Barb included.

"You can't drive us, ma'am?" the woman called after me.

I stopped walking, then turned to face her, but only her.

"To where," I said.

"Chinatown," The Money Man said.

"Chinatown," Barb said, "would be more like a vacation."

I pictured five one hundred dollar bills on my palm. I'd invested time into this deal, and I didn't want to park The Reliant in Manhattan—or anywhere—ever again. And to stop Barb's whining, I'd have to buy her five pale ales. Hearing the swish of the street sweeper, I said, "Fine," and Barb asked, "Do restaurants in Chinatown serve breakfast?"

"Get in the car," I said. "Everyone."

The Mechanic tried to open a locked door, and the handle slipped from his fingertips.

"He's not going to buy it," Barb said. "He just wants a free ride home."

"He's going to buy it," the woman said.

"Yeah, Barb," I said. "Quit being so mistrustful." I unlocked The Reliant's doors, and Barb got in on the front passenger side and gazed out her window, looking, in yesterday's hair and those brown corduroys, like a hitchhiker who'd slept under a bridge.

The Money Man followed The Mechanic into the back, and the woman followed them, and I, feeling suddenly like the mother of their family, took my place behind the wheel.

The engine fired up as obediently as ever. I signaled and pulled out, my homemade contracts crackling in my pocket. I faked a glance over my shoulder and turned down Columbus and said, "I assume we simply go south?"

"We go to Chinatown," The Money Man said.

"We take this man home," Barb said.

"Can you work on your people skills, Barb?" I said, and, to vent my frustration—with her, with the cost of living in Manhattan, with my tendency to think when most people simply act—I accelerated. The pothole was visible at the very last second, and then it was under me, and then I heard what sounded like an explosion, and I struggled, with all of my arm-strength, to keep The Reliant on the asphalt. Its steering wheel locked into a sharp pull to the left, and its insides moaned, and its left bumper missed a parked car by six inches, then another by three. A hair from the curb, aimed at pedestrians and a sidewalk cafe, it stopped.

I opened my door two inches—as far as it went. Red liquid pooled beside the curb. Blown transmission, I thought, remembering an alcoholic uncle of mine once saying those words to my father. And the jolt had shoved the front part of the car over the door. I looked over my shoulder: my new family did little but watch me and blink. Behind them, I noticed through the grit-tinted rear window, was a trail of the red liquid—and a bald guy in a BE ALL YOU CAN BE sweatshirt waving a hubcap over his head. He ran to my door, tried to open it beyond the two inches, then knocked on my roof.

I rolled down my window and said, "Hello, sir."

"Don't worry," he said, shoving the hubcap toward my face. "I chased it for you."

"Thanks," I said, and I took the hubcap. "But I don't think I'll need it."

"Next stop's the junkyard?" he asked.

"Exactly," I said. "And after that, some godforsaken place like El *Paso* where I can afford rent."

"Relax," Barb said. "You probably just blew out a tire."

"Look behind you, Barb," I said, and Barb grunted as she turned, a very bad time to remind us our torsos had lost their youthful flexibility.

"Transmission fluid," she said. Her eyebrows fought a smirk. "And the guy didn't sign your contract."

"You think that's funny?" I asked, and her face threatened to sprout a smile.

"Possibly," she said.

"Like you enjoy the fact that Thom's dating that Pilates freak while I'm here without anyone."

She shrugged, and I considered telling her right then and there about the plastic vagina, but now she was laughing freely, and I thought better of it.

"This isn't funny," the bald guy said.

"Exactly," I said. "This car was supposed to be my next month's rent."

"I'm sorry," he said.

"Not your fault," I told him.

"Listen," he said. "You mind if I take your battery?"

"Not in the least," I said, and I yanked the hood latch handle under the dash and took the only tool I owned, a screwdriver Thom and I bought to replace a headlight we finally paid a neighbor to fix, from the glove box. "Take whatever you want," I said.

"Seriously?" he asked.

I nodded and handed him the screwdriver. Barb opened her door and got out, and I followed her through the passenger side, despising her brown corduroys and beer-inflated hips.

Columbus Avenue was crowded, and Barb walked toward a tavern that may or may not have been open and didn't appear safe, no doubt to pursue one of her "rough-morning-exception" drinks. *Let* her become an alcoholic, I thought, and I poked my head back into the car, where my family continued to sit.

"You can leave now," I told them. "You're off the hook."

They looked at one another, then, one at a time, at me.

"If you don't go now," I said, "I might yell at you."

The Money Man glanced at my boobs. I rolled my eyes and opened the back door for his sister.

"Your brother can still buy the car," I said as she slid out, and The Money Man shook his head no. He stepped into the street, beside the woman, as did The Mechanic. Then traffic rushed toward us, and I considered mentioning this, but our zone of safety was shrinking quickly, so I shoved them past the trunk to the sidewalk. Then I walked to the open hood and watched the bald guy unscrew my battery. I touched The Reliant for the sake of future sentiment, then noticed, near a cafe table on the sidewalk, the Chinese people standing side by side. As suddenly as they'd felt like my family, they were now obviously not, but they were watching me, maybe to see if I, like The Reliant, would break down.

To prevent that from happening, I helped the bald guy remove whatever accouterments he could, including the license plates and the floor mats, and I piled what he'd taken beside the curb. Then the same cop who'd appeared on 76th pulled up and told me I could get fined for leaving a stripped car on the street, as well as for not "retiring" my license plates.

"Can't I just leave the plates on?" I asked. "This is hard enough as it is, and—"

"The mob likes to sell abandoned plates. You don't want to be involved in a mess like that."

"I guess not," I said, and I snatched the damned license plates off the pile. "I'll have the car towed."

"Won't cost you as much as a fine," he said, and he sped off, and I crossed the street toward Barb's most recently discovered dive. Its air-conditioning exhaust smelled like her apartment had on the mornings after she'd thrown all-night parties (before she'd met Dwayne); inside, she was stirring the ice cubes of an all-but-consumed Bloody Mary with one of those little red straws, sitting at the end of the bar closest to the door, a precaution, I guessed, against what the two hard-cores at the other end might try. I sat beside her, set the license plates on the bar, and said, "You missed a second chance to have sex with that cop."

"What's that supposed to mean?" she asked.

"I don't know. Just keeping you informed."

The bartender glanced at me, and I ordered a straight orange juice, which he served. I asked for a yellow pages, and he went into a back room to look.

"Why the yellow pages?" Barb asked between sips.

"I have to call a junk dealer. Or get fined."

She didn't say anything, just swigged at her ice cubes.

"I don't think this is funny, Barb," I said.

"I never said it was."

"But you were smiling out there. Right after I...hit the pothole."

"I did not smile."

"Okay. You smirked."

"Can't a person *smirk*?"

"Not in a situation like this. Not if she's a friend."

"Then I don't know what to tell you," she said.

"Meaning what?"

She made several loud slurping noises through her straw.

"Okay, Barb. Let's just get this all out. I'm *endlessly* sorry about the Dwayne thing. But I want to make one fact clear. All he and I did was *spoon*. And I'll be honest with you: if you aren't over that by now, you have problems, one of which might be that you and just about everyone we know in Kankakee drinks too much."

"I'm *way* over the spooning," she said. "In fact, I broke up with Dwayne the day you left town. And if you want to be honest, I'll tell you why I smirked."

"Go ahead."

She set down her glass and locked her eyes on mine. "Everyone in Kankakee," she said, "knows you won't last in this city. In fact, quite a few of us are making bets about when you'll be back. So it's just kind of amusing that your car, you know, exploded."

"*You* made a bet?"

She nodded. "And it looks like I'll win."

"That's cold, Barb."

"You wanted to know."

"I'm not talking about telling me. I'm talking about making the bet."

"Hey," she said. "I *know* you. Is that such a crime?"

"All you know is what you've been told," I said, unaware then that if I stayed in New York, I'd know more—about men, women, and crime—than I would ever like to admit.

Chapter 4

Barb's stay taught me at least three lessons: 1) she hadn't wanted to see me as much as use me for a free place to stay while she toured an expensive city; 2) after you leave the Midwest, people talk about you more than they did when you lived there; 3) when *two* pairs of Letterman tickets arrived in the mail the day before my rent was due, I was living on luck.

And with those tickets in hand it became easier to put my Kankakee friends behind me, since I had work to do. The first pair took an entire hour to sell, but after I found a woman with a daughter who seemed more fond of Dave than I was (the daughter was so jazzed by the tickets, she actually kissed me), they brought $175 apiece. The second pair took even longer to sell, because it hit me that, for the sake of optimal profit margin, I should approach only people who looked the most put-together, but I finally found a grandfather from Oklahoma with diamond rings on most of his fingers, and he pulled out a wad of hundreds and said, "How 'bout I give you four of these?"

Even better, only three days later, I got a care package from an aunt I barely knew, and inside was *her* pair of tickets, which told me that, as long as I kept mailing requests to the Ed Sullivan Theater, I not only could afford rent, I might also have my own thriving business. I immediately bought a Day-Runner and scheduled days when I'd mail requests, then made a list of people to whom the requests would go, including dozens of acquaintances I hadn't seen since high school. I reminisced now and then as I made this list, and sometimes, when I'd receive tickets from someone I'd probably never see again, I worried that I was a user.

But it was good and easy money, most of the time $150 a ticket, enough for me to make it in Manhattan on my own modest terms. Now and then I even had cash to hear bands downtown, where I met streams of hip people, artists and writers and actors. And I don't mean wannabes; these people actually supported themselves with careers people in the Midwest would never fathom. For example this guy Luke, who designed perfume bottles. That was his *whole* job. If a cosmetics company were planning a new perfume, they'd give him twenty grand minimum to sketch a few designs for the bottle whether they'd use his ideas or not—because everyone who mattered knew he was *the* perfume bottle design guy. And if someone used his design? Fifty grand. It didn't hurt his cause that he had an Italian accent, with which he could talk most anyone's pants off. He had mine off once, but then he fell asleep, leaving me awake on his bed with thoughts about Thom and Barb and Dwayne—and the conclusion that, as impersonal as Manhattan sometimes felt, I never wanted to see Kankakee again. Maybe Luke was overworked that night, or too drunk to do what he would have done otherwise.

Or maybe I was too drunk. He did give me a look while we were at a club earlier that night, possibly suggesting, it seemed, that I was talking about myself too much. I asked Etta about that, and she said I could be "loquacious." But I was honest, she said. She also mentioned that, when she'd been my age, she'd learned the hard way to watch her tongue in the city, and when I asked her what she meant by the hard way, she didn't answer, just re-told her story about the two widowed people who rendezvoused after all those years, changing a fact or two as usual. Etta might have been the slightest bit senile, but if so it showed only when she was near sleep in her tub.

And she never lost her composure until I met a heart surgeon named Del and stayed at his place for three days; she became what I'd call disproportionately upset about that. I'd shopped for a boatload of groceries the afternoon before I met this guy, so she'd had enough food to take her through World War III, and, yes, there was Tino, but Tino could relieve himself in the little yard behind her building, and when I say three days, I mean only two nights—and, yes, it's good to bathe daily, but it's not like you'll die if you don't. And here I was, possibly falling in *love*, with a man who wasn't just one of those jerks who says he's a heart surgeon but turns out to be a pharmacist, and after our first night together, he got all boyish and said something was telling him to marry me. And I didn't tell him to take things slowly, just gave him a look that let him know I already felt serious too, and we spent the rest of that day sipping champagne and making love and doing things teenage lovers would do, like tickling each other's necks. Don't get me wrong: our behavior had me baffled. But after hearing Etta's story about that old happy couple, I didn't want to ruin what could be a once-in-a-lifetime chance by playing it off.

You'd think, then, that Etta would have understood, but she didn't. On the night after my three days away, I even told her I loved Del, and I've never told anyone that I've loved anyone else, not even my father when I'd been dating Thom, but she just complained about how I'd gone back on our deal. She also scolded me about the clothes on the floor in my room, which she'd never gone into before those three days, and I wanted to tell her I expected my room to be private, but I didn't since it was clear she could always find someone else to bathe her and walk Tino: no lease said I could live with her forever. Instead, I waited until the next evening—after Tino was walked—then took the N downtown to see Del.

But Del wasn't home. And he never was after that. I called the number he'd given me, and his voice was on the machine but he didn't pick up, and I left a message saying I'd stopped by, but he didn't call back. I rolled with his silence for six days, because now, for the sake of our future, I thought it best not to seem infatuated, and then I phoned him again and left a message that included Etta's number, but he never returned that call either. I cabbed to his building on four more occasions, buzzing up to his place a dozen times apiece, but nothing came of it. Except for just after I buzzed up the very last time, when I left his building and saw him standing at the end of his block facing a perfectly tall (non-Amazon) woman with dewy cheekbones and Prada everything. Anyone could see they had a thing for each other, because as they talked they absolutely ignored passersby, and she kept training her hair behind her ears, and he kept holding back his shoulders for the sake of posture. It was love if I've ever seen it, which meant what he'd said to me about marriage now made me feel stupid, to the point that I didn't want him to notice me. Then I couldn't help myself, and I headed toward them to see if my proximity would cause him to say hello. He noticed me approach—we had fluid but definite eye contact—but when I was ten feet away, he feigned a kick at a pebble, apparently saying something witty just before he did, because she chuckled, grabbing his forearm. I stood directly beside him as I pretended to wait for a green light to allow me to cross 23rd Street, but he ignored me, and I remembered how, during our first night together, he said he found me "spontaneous," which I now took to mean that, around him, I hadn't thought *enough*.

Finally, after he laughed in response to a shrug of hers, they walked off together, in the opposite direction of his building, and as I began across 23rd in earnest, I wondered whether they were headed toward her place, but the only truly important issue was whether or not to let Etta know what a loser I was. I knew it was emotionally healthy to tell someone when you've been used for sex, if for no other reason than to get your newest level of frustration about men off your chest, but to do this with Etta would more or less require that I apologize to her for letting her down.

And I hate to apologize. Whenever I do it, I feel as if I'm handing the person a pair of steel-toed boots and saying, "Use these to walk all over me." Thom used to say that a quick apology was the easiest way to keep a small misunderstanding from becoming a full-blown yelling match followed by yet another all-night *discussion about the relationship*, and when he and I had gotten along, I'd agreed with this theory of his, but whenever it was my turn to apologize, I would have preferred to extract my own teeth. I don't know. I'm not perfect. Which is something that, once you admit it, should make apologies easier—unless your worst imperfection is that you hate to apologize.

The more I mulled all of this over on my way uptown, the more twisted I felt, and at some point I decided that maybe the best reason in general to apologize is to stop yourself from having to think. I also realized that the best manner to apologize is with the written word (so you won't blush or get tongue-tied or possibly cry), so I stopped off at a drugstore on Eighth Avenue to buy Etta a card. For a while in front of the card rack, I searched for something with a pre-composed all-purpose apology for me—all I'd have to do was sign—but either the store didn't stock cards like that, or they were all gone. Finally I found an eggshell white card with a sketched daisy on the front and blank insides, and it cost four dollars but I took it anyway, telling myself I was paying for my imperfections but that the card was therefore worth it, and after I got home and went straight to my room without seeing Etta, I wrote "Sorry" inside the card, then signed my first name. For a solid half an hour, I debated about whether I should wedge "& Love" beside the "Sorry" (what if Etta would think the person I really loved was Del?), but then I crammed it in there, found her in the kitchen doing dishes, handed the card to her, walked back into my room, and closed the door.

I'd sat on my bed for just under three heartbeats when she knocked. It seemed to take all my energy to step to the door and open it, and after I did, she leveled me with a stern expression, then said, "Forgiven"   and walked off.

And when I bathed her that night, she was as nice as ever, telling me she'd thought of a surprise for me that would help me keep my room neat, then singing her Norwegian songs as if, between me and her, all that had ever happened was kindness.

Chapter 5

The following night, while Etta was in Brooklyn visiting her sister, I was returning from smoking a cigarette in the back yard with Tino, and I walked into my
room to find a redheaded woman standing there, holding a duffel bag. At least
fifty years old, she'd gone overboard with foundation to hide the freckles on her
nose, but you could still see the cuteness she must have had as a child. "Ernest,"
she said, "is in the living room."

"Pardon?" I said, because I'd never met an Ernest.

"Your super," she said. I was sure she was wearing a Wonderbra. "Etta
asked him to build a loft for you. He's in the living room, and I think he's napping in there."

"Okay," I said for lack of something better, and she glanced at the doorway
still open behind me, so I turned and saw, standing on the threshold, a man
maybe seventy years old, at least six feet tall, and pear-shaped: narrow, sloping
shoulders that, from one end to the other, measured maybe half the width of his

hips. He wore relaxed fit jeans, a red Izod sport shirt like the one I'd bought at a Goodwill in 1989, and a purple silk ascot that failed to completely hide the fact that a chunk of his jawbone was missing.

"Ernest?" I asked as I completed an unintended double take.

He nodded, then pulled a notepad from his back pocket.

"Ernest can't speak," the redheaded woman said, and Ernest sidled to my left and elbowed my forearm, writing on the pad with a pencil not even as long as his thumb. He tore off the sheet and handed it to me. His printing was large, a lot like mine in fifth grade:

MICHELLE?

"Yes," I said, and he blinked at me, and I nodded—as if he couldn't hear. We shook hands, his so big my fingers felt absorbed into it, the hand, I thought, of a home builder or dockworker, though the skin on his palm was loose and smooth. "My pleasure," I said. He smiled and nodded in an exaggerated way that suggested he preferred not to jot down small talk.

"Should we tell her?" the woman asked, and I wondered: Tell who what?

Ernest wrote more, then tore off the sheet, walked past me, and handed what he'd written to the woman. As she read, her lips moved so slowly I couldn't read them. She crumpled the sheet and dropped it into the wastebasket Etta had bought for me. "Ernest," she said, "used to play baseball."

"Oh," I said, intrigued by her apparent comfort with non-sequiturs. "My ex played baseball," I said to smooth this one over. "In high school."

"You're not following," she said. "Ernest played for the Yankees. For half of a season, he led the team in triples."

Right, I thought. This man, in this Izod, played professional baseball.

"People still stop him on the street," she said.

"I'm sure they do," I said.

"He calls himself Ernest Coolridge," the woman said. "But he's not really

Ernest Coolridge. You know what I'm saying?"

I nodded, and Ernest—who I then secretly and facetiously named The Great Yank—began scribbling on his pad. He crossed a T, then tapped the rounded tip of his pencil under his message:

> DON'T MIND
> JOYCE.
>
> SHE LIKES TO TELL
> STORIES.

I thought about reading this out loud, thought again, then smiled, and he smiled back, and the crookedness of his mouth, which conveyed discomfort, made me wonder if he, rather than Joyce, was the bullshitter. After all, I told myself, plenty of famous people choose to avoid public exposure for the sake of sanity. The speechlessness and the problem with the left side of his face could be explained, I figured, by some kind of throat-and-jaw cancer surgery necessitated by a habit of chewing tobacco, as well as the possibility that he, without the pressure of public exposure—without sports agents, p.r. experts, and eager plastic surgeons—decided, maybe for health reasons, against reconstruction. I was all set to talk to him as if I weren't affected by these possibilities (in other words, play it as casually as I could) when the lights in the room flickered.

"Shit," Joyce said.

Then the lights went out altogether. I heard traffic outside the window, but nothing else, no music from Etta's radio in the living room, no refrigerator hum from down the hall: we'd lost power.

"Find a candle, Ernest," Joyce said, and to make sense of what I'd seen and heard so far, I theorized that The Great Yank had met her toward the end of his days as a womanizing baseball player   maybe just before the cancer-of-the-throat-and-jaw surgery—and, in the process, fallen in love.

Theory aside, his ability to inhale was in trouble as he opened the top drawer of the bureau I shared with Etta's china and silver. He was obeying the command to find the candle, it seemed, and his breaths sounded like those of someone victimized by strangulation, and I was bombarded, as I listened to them and his rifling through Etta's silverware, with memories of the asthma I'd had as a kid. I remembered the horror of how breathlessness can appear and try to cling—and his wheezing fell silent.

"Ernest?" Joyce said. "Are you all right?"

I pictured The Great Yank rolling his eyes at his obvious inability to answer. Then I feared what Joyce might be fearing—that he was lying at our feet, passed out. I reached in front of me to take a step, and my palm pressed against the knot of his ascot, my fingers confirming that half of his jawbone was gone.

"Sorry," I said as I pulled back my hand.

"For what?" Joyce asked.

"I'm talking to Ernest," I said. "I, uh, touched him."

"For God's sake, we need a candle," she said.

Fingernails tickled my back. His? I wondered, and I heard more rifling. "Does Etta keep candles in here, Ernest?" Joyce asked, now near the bureau: the fingernails, I decided, had been hers as she'd passed me to get there.

Then something squeaked at the other end of the room, the ascent of my room-darkening shade. Nightfall had covered Manhattan, so the window allowed in just enough indirect orange streetlight to silhouette The Great Yank's head, neck, and shoulders. Now that I could study that part of him without worrying about being caught, I saw that his left shoulder was not merely sloped; it was gone, like the ghosted half of his jawbone, and he was walking toward the window—had the shade, I wondered, risen by itself?—stepping on a strewn blouse of mine, then climbing onto the windowsill using the wobbly silver radiator as a step. Then he was up there, on the sill, tiptoed, facing the pane, steadying himself by spreading his arms to pinch both sides of the window frame with his fingertips, and Joyce said, "Changing the fuse won't help, Ernest."

He sidestepped toward the left side of the frame.

"Ernest?" Joyce said. "Did you hear me?"

He offered two exaggerated nods, then reached for the ceiling.

"Stand behind him," Joyce told me. "So he doesn't fall backwards."

Or forwards, I thought. Headed toward him, I tripped over the wastebasket, and he glanced at me over his missing shoulder. "I'm okay," I said, and I stepped behind him and reached over my own head, my hands spread the width of his atrophied butt cheeks, my fingers poised either to catch him or grab his belt loop—and possibly join him if he crashed through the window.

"I'm telling you, Ernest," Joyce said. "A new fuse won't help an iota."

The Great Yank's breathing hissed until, without turning around, he gave Joyce the finger. I had to admit I agreed with her—what good was a fuse when the whole building was void of power?—but I admired his spunk in this particular round of the battle of the sexes. He pulled down the shade, let it rise, pulled it down, let it rise. A sheet of streetlight hung over my bed. He took his notepad from his shirt pocket and the tiny pencil from behind his ear, then wrote slowly, his balance just steady enough. Then he tore the message off the pad and lowered it toward my face.

THE SHADE IS
BROKEN.

GET ME A FORK.

"What," Joyce said.

"He wants a fork," I said.

"You don't change a fuse with a fork."

"He says the shade's broken," I said, although, from my experience, broken shades were victories for planned obsolescence.

"Forget the shade, Ernest," Joyce said. "The shade hardly matters with the lights out at night."

The Great Yank shot a look at me and snapped his fingers twice, and I walked, avoiding the wastebasket, to the bureau.

"Don't give him a fork," Joyce said.

I cleared my throat. "He said he wanted it."

"You can't do whatever he wants just because he used to play baseball."

He *was* a Yankee, I thought, and I allowed a shiver to settle into me. I groped in the drawer, found a fork, then walked it back to his hand telling myself that from then on, to help myself relax around him, I should call him nothing more than Ernest.

His breathing was better. "The faster he fixes the shade," I told Joyce, "the faster he'll fix the lights."

He unhooked the shade, then used a space between fork tines as a wrench on the tiny metal rectangle on the end of the shade's wooden dowel, cranking it counterclockwise.

"I think I smell smoke," Joyce said, and she was right. And it wasn't from cigarettes, either. It smelled like a campfire. Ernest must smell it, I thought, and he kept cranking the fork handle, and this calmed me: he seemed like one of those ultra-experienced men who, in all situations, knew what he was doing. And since he'd been a Yankee, I didn't want his first impression of me to be the impetuous kook who'd said "fire" and begun a false alarm.

Then I remembered something I'd noticed the day I'd moved in with Etta— the spouts of her building's sprinkler system had been gummed up by what appeared to be at least three coats of paint—and my own breathing began to feel compromised.

"I'm going downstairs," Joyce said. "To see where it's coming from."

I wanted to speak for Ernest to answer her, but she left. Then, from Ernest's silence, I learned a valuable lesson: bitching by one's lover is best addressed quickly, then ignored. He hung the shade and pulled it down, returning us to darkness. "Fixed," I said as he stepped to the floor, and the shade, with both of us standing some six feet from it, rose an inch. "Dammit," I said, and I wondered if speaking for him was causing me to feel what he felt.

"We're not going to burn," Joyce called from the doorway. "A guy from the second floor said smoke descends," she continued, "so if there *is* a fire, it's coming from the roof. Which means we won't have a problem getting out."

Smoke descends? I thought. "The guy really said that?" I asked.

"Yeah," Joyce said. "I saw him on the stairs."

"He just checked the roof?"

"I don't know."

I coughed. "Don't you think someone should check it?"

"Let me ask you something, missy. Have you lived in the city for a good part of your life?"

"Yes," I said, which wasn't entirely false, because the fraction of my life spent in the city had felt better than any other.

"And you never smelled smoke in a building?"

"Not like this."

"Then you haven't lived here long enough."

A strip of streetlight revealed a grimace on Ernest's face. He was slouched on my bed and, given several grunts and the direction of his eyes, re-tying his shoes. He gestured his notepad toward my hand. I took it and used the light to read:

> LET'S GET
> OUT
> OF HERE.

"What," Joyce said.

"He's leaving," I said.

"If you think there's a fire, Ernest," she said, "take your duffel bag."

Then the door creaked, and I groped for the doorway, found it without touching Joyce, and followed the sound of footsteps down the hall. "Ernest?" Joyce's voice called from behind us.

The footsteps led me down the smoke-filled staircase. Wooden, I remembered as I descended, and my throat constricted, and I coughed. Finally I saw hazy orange light—the ground floor—and then we were out, coughing on the sidewalk, Ernest and I. His shoes, I noticed, were Air Jordans.

"You didn't bring your duffel bag?" I asked.

He pulled his notepad from his front pocket and scribbled.

I JUST WANTED
TO
BREATHE.

"Oh," I said.

AND I'M NOT
TALKING
ABOUT THE SMOKE,
EITHER.

"You don't think there's a fire?"

He shook his head, and I nodded to show I understood, maybe unintentionally causing him to believe that I agreed, and he held my elbow to lead me across the street, and, for a moment there, with part of me again feeling absorbed into him, I would have gone anywhere he wanted. Then we stood side by side, facing Etta's building. Roughly six blocks from us, I knew from my Letterman radar, was the Ed Sullivan Theater, and I pictured myself sitting in Dave's studio audience, Dave flirting with me on national TV. What if Dave likes you? I thought, and I heard a siren approach. Wanting to tell Joyce that I knew sirens were as meaningless as smoke, I searched the ground floor windows of the building for signs of flames. Then a fire engine rounded the corner and stopped to the right of the building, and firemen armed with extinguishers, axes, and packets of sunflower seeds completed a semi-enthused march toward the door. Two of them pushed buttons to buzz up and another spat seeds as Ernest wrote on his pad:

A PRECAUTION.

"A precaution," I said too loudly. I believed I was feeling what Ernest felt, overall calmness mildly salted with panic. I wondered if this new skill of mine— the ability to put into words what others were feeling—was the key to being hip in Manhattan. "Listen," I said to him to divert my eyes from the firemen. "I think I know who you are," I said, which was an outright lie because I knew less about baseball than I did about, say, Saudi Arabian history. "And I'm hoping you can answer a question."

He flashed the okay sign.

"Aside from being a sports hero, how does a person make it in the city?"

He smirked and hunkered down on his pad.

MAKE EVERYONE
HAPPY.

"But everyone says you *can't* make everyone happy."

I DID.

"But that was a different era," I said. "I mean, everything is different now, don't you think?"

IF SO,
I WON'T LAST

HERE MUCH

LONGER.

And I won't either? I wondered.

"One more question," I said. "If you don't mind?"

HIT ME.

"What's it like to be famous?"

He raised one finger, telling me, I was sure, that his answer would be worth my wait and his effort. He wrote hard, blinking repeatedly, then handed over the notepad.

FAME

FINALLY

EXHAUSTS YOU.

The ground floor window under my room exploded, glass raining onto the sidewalk. Smoke twisted out and rose.

"Joyce better leave," I said.

Ernest wrote:

FIRE ESCAPE

IN BACK.

"Good," I said, and he nodded, and I did, too, and I was glad Tino was in Etta's section of the building's back yard: with the firemen now inside, I trusted he'd be safe there. Then I wasn't so sure. To distract myself from worry, I asked Ernest, "What was in your duffel bag?"

MEMORABILIA.
I WAS
GOING TO
SELL IT.

Another window exploded, and then they were exploding from left to right, ax-heads popping through them like iron tongues. This is serious, I almost said, but the escaping smoke tapered off. Then axes shattered two second-floor windows. I glanced at Ernest, whose eyes were fixed on the window to my room, and his expression assured me that he, unlike Joyce, knew that heat and smoke ascended, and that he was picturing Joyce dashing through Etta's dark hallway while his duffel bag remained beside a bra on my floor.

"Excuse me," I told him.

I crossed the street, accelerated toward the building, and a fireman yelled, "*Ma'am. Where you going?*"

"I've got to get something," I said. "Just a duffel bag. Before it burns."

"It's burning."

"What if it's still there?"

"It's burning. You might as well phone your insurance."

"I can't run up and check?"

"We just got everyone out of there. You run up and I lose my job." He clutched an industrial-size crowbar. "So you're not running up."

I nodded and walked back to Ernest. We stood beside each other, neither speaking nor writing, just watching more onslaughts of smoke. Then a hand squeezed my shoulder hard enough to portend rudeness. Joyce? I thought, and I turned and saw Etta pulled up as close to my left as Ernest was to my right.

"Etta," I said, "can you believe this?"

"Unfortunately," she said.

"At least we're out here," I said, but my insides churned—because if the third floor caught fire, our living arrangement might end. "Tino's out back," I said. "In the yard."

Ernest thickened a period and handed his notepad to me, and Etta read it as I did:

I HOPE

JOYCE

BRINGS

MY DUFFEL

BAG.

"So do I," I said.

"What was in his duffel bag?" Etta asked me, and before I could answer, another fire truck rounded the corner. Ernest and I exchanged glances. He shrugged. Then the second-floor window beneath mine exploded without the help of an ax. Inside that room, the tips of flames stretched into view. Ernest's breathing grew vexed, then worse. He had only so much memorabilia, I was sure, and he was probably picturing his last aged and genuine baseball singe, and his autograph on that baseball could have made someone happy—and helped Ernest afford more of the city. I felt sorry for the person the memorabilia might have made happy, and for Ernest himself. I felt ashamed that I'd fanta-sized about Letterman while Ernest's future had burned.

"If the whole building goes," I said to myself out loud, and then I babbled about how I'd just begun to get my life together, about how Manhattan was the only place open enough to let me be who I really was, and about who knows what else. As I said these things, I used phrases made common on talk shows and felt destined to make an awful impression on Ernest, but I babbled on anyway, and then I tried to explain to Ernest that, for most of my life (which, granted, I added, had been less than half of his), all of my trying and talking and lovemaking and understanding had done nothing but separate me from everyone else. Then I noticed that his breathing had gone silent, and I turned to see his pencil finish a message:

> I KNOW
> WHAT YOU
> MEAN.

"Do you really?"

He nodded, sat on the curb, and watched the flames rise. Then he lay back so that his legs were splayed on the street, his spine flat against a sidewalk dotted by black, discarded gum. He shut his eyes and placed his palms down, one on top of the other, on his chest.

"Will you *watch* it?" I yelled at a woman who nearly stepped on his head, but she kept on walking, so I hoped for a response from Ernest.

His eyes stayed shut. He can't, I thought, handle the city right now.

"Ernest?" I tried.

Someone tapped my shoulder: Joyce, hugging Tino, then handing him to Etta. "Ernest is napping," she said. "He does this wherever he feels."

Etta glanced over. "Is he okay?" she asked me.

"I'd say he's felt better," I said.

"I took CPR at the gym," a guy on the sidewalk behind us said. "If anyone here can help, it's me." This guy was huge, maybe three hundred pounds, and he planted his feet on either side of Ernest's chest, then crouched so his ass touched Ernest's abdomen, then rested on it.

"And I'm engaged to this man," Joyce said. "Do you see what I have to put up with?"

"You're smothering him," I told the fat guy.

"I'm helping him," he said.

"I don't think so," I said. "He doesn't need CPR. It's a *breathing* thing."

He placed a palm on Ernest's chest and pressed. "It's his heart," he said, and I grabbed his gargantuan arm and tried to shove him off of Ernest, but he didn't budge. I pushed again, using strength I hadn't expected, and he let go of Ernest's dwindled shoulders and rolled onto the sidewalk. He was lying beside Ernest, straining to sit up, but I didn't see him rise: I was hovering over Ernest, pinching his nose and grabbing the skin where his jaw was supposed to be, and lowering the flabby remains of his chin.

Then I was descending, hoping Ernest's eyes would open before our lips touched. Then we were sharing his silence. His mouth was warm, and I exhaled into it, and my palm, on his chest, rose slightly. I won't have to do this more than twice, I thought, and I inhaled, tasting garlic, halitosis, and cinnamon. I heard glass pelt the sidewalk across the street. I tried not to hear the fat guy, who was shouting at me with instructions. One more time, I told myself, and I'll hear that troubled breathing. Everything will be exactly the way it was.

I exhaled into him again, but he didn't respond, and then *I* struggled to breathe, and I imagined myself dead but wasn't especially horrified. I wouldn't say I wanted to die, just that, for a rush of moments as I exhaled into him a third time, death right there felt almost acceptable, maybe because I might have departed heroically—*Kankakee Woman Revives Beloved Yankee.*

Then, as I inhaled, I felt pressure in his nostrils, and I let go of his nose and watched his face grow pale yet twitch, as if his death and life continued to fight. Lying still, he blinked at the corridor of sky above us, then sat up, faced me, and mouthed the words *I'm sorry.* He patted his pockets and found his notepad. His handwriting this time was larger than before, a detail I interpreted as emphasis:

REALLY.

I'M

SORRY

THAT HAPPENED.

"Don't be," I said, and Joyce eyed me like a statue, her nonverbal declaration that she'd prefer I keep my relatively young breasts away from her man.

Whether she knew he'd left the duffel bag in the building was debatable. Then he flipped his apology behind the other used pages of his notebook, jotted on a fresh one, and showed it to her, and she said, "No, Ernest. I thought you brought it. In fact, I told you to bring it."

He didn't bother to answer, but his troubled breathing returned. It hadn't helped that, while he and I had shared breathlessness, another fire truck had arrived, though no flames were visible, just crow-black smoke rolling out of the windows on the first and second floors. The third-floor windows, including mine, were still intact.

"Ernest?" Joyce said. "Did you hear me?"

He nodded without facing her. He watched the third floor as if willing Etta's apartment to survive. His eyes pierced, something I'd noticed when we'd shaken hands in my room but ignored to keep us platonic. Now there was also hope in his eyes, or maybe I was reading hope into them because I couldn't see a fireman anywhere, just a fat khaki hose attached to a hydrant and stretched through the building's propped-open front doorway: all of the firemen were inside, being firemen.

"Troubling," Etta said. She and Tino were behind me, Joyce to her right, Ernest maybe three feet to my left. The fat guy, I realized, was gone. A few pedestrians stood watching, but less like they cared than like they were trying to avoid arriving someplace early. Passersby remained stone-faced except to express annoyance with having to cross the street.

Like Ernest, I tried to let myself hope. I imagined the flames and smoke gone, as well as a battalion chief escorting me to my unburned room, pointing at my clothes on the floor, and saying, "*This* is a freaking hazard." Then an ax burst through my bedroom window, broken glass raining onto the sidewalk across the street, and smoke pressed toward me through the jagged hole.

Chapter 6

I spent the rest of the night standing on that sidewalk, more or less knowing what the verdict would be, yet watching fire, police, and insurance people do what they do between the departure of the last fire truck and the moment they decide if the yellow tape cris-crossed over the door will come down and residents will be allowed inside. After a neighbor took Tino to her studio on 48th, Ernest and Etta and I and even Joyce teamed up to help each other think positively, though mostly through silent refusal to look away from the building, since whatever we'd say rang hollow. At some point it seemed obvious that Ernest and Joyce were trying not to think about his memorabilia, and Etta was trying not to think about her apartment, and I was trying not to think about how my quasi-friend Barb might still win her bet.

Then a Red Cross worker strolled across 49th and introduced herself as Darcy, and told us that some head inspector still hadn't decided whether tenants could return to the building, but that volunteers had set up cots in a high school gym in Hell's Kitchen for anyone whose I.D. confirmed proof of residency in the building, which she said she needed because it wasn't uncommon for people to show up at fires and say they lived in the burnt buildings to swindle the Red Cross. I told her I didn't have an I.D. because I'd left my purse inside (all I had in there was my Illinois driver's license, but I kept that fact secret), though Etta had an electric bill stub in her purse, and she vouched for me, so Darcy believed me, "pending confirmation."

At around four in the morning, Etta and I walked to the high school, where volunteers offered us turkey and cheese sandwiches, bottled water, and "comfort kits." My comfort kit was just a tiny washcloth, a trial-size tube of toothpaste, a toothbrush, and a comb, but I'm not complaining, because when we got to the gym, I needed in the worst way to wash my face.

Despite a cot I'd claimed in a corner, I didn't sleep, or even try. Etta lay down for a while, mostly with her eyes open. Then she dozed, or at least I think she did, and three or four other golden agers from our building were trying to sleep there, too, and I sat on a folding chair beneath the electric scoreboard and, more than a decade after I'd been in a school, decided that what bothered me most about them was their smell.

Then I couldn't handle waiting there for official word about Etta's building, so I walked back to 49th. Joyce was gone, but Ernest was there. Police, as well as what I guessed were arson investigators, were still ducking under the yellow tape to walk inside and out.

"Any news?" I asked Ernest after we nodded hellos, and he removed his note-pad from his shirt pocket as noises from his throat betrayed his impatience—or anger. Then he wrote:

HEAVY DAMAGE.

"That's what they told you?"

I PROVED
I WAS THE
SUPER
& THEY LET ME
IN.
(BRIEFLY.)

"Totally burned?" I asked, and, far more slowly than I could remain patient, he wrote:

BETWEEN THE
FIRE & WHAT
THEY DID WITH
THE HATCHETS,
I WOULDN'T
BET ON A ROOM
WITHOUT
A LOFT.

"Shit," I said, and I might have cried right then if everything hadn't seemed so unbelievable.

I'M SORRY,
MICHELLE.

"Not your fault," I said, and he cocked his head and raised his eyebrows, as if letting on that, as the building's super, he harbored an untoward secret about it—like, say, it hadn't been up to code—but I told myself this couldn't be true, and that, if it were, there had probably been only so much he could have done about it. Then I realized he might have been mourning the loss of his memorabilia, and I felt so damned selfish for forgetting about that, I almost didn't want to ask about it. He was fidgety, though, his way, I imagined, of dealing with the burden of some bottom line of unshared thought, so I blurted, "What about your duffel bag?"

He held up a finger, then wrote:

SOMEONE
TOOK IT.

"You're kidding," I said.

MY GUESS: AN
INSURANCE GUY.

"Then *I'm* sorry," I said. "Because it was kind of my fault you left it there. I mean, if I hadn't been a slob, Etta wouldn't have asked you to build a loft in my room, and..."

He wrote quickly:

QUE SERA.

Then he reached into his pants pocket and pulled out a folded envelope and handed it to me. As I unfolded it, I recognized the blue type of the Ed Sullivan Theater's return address: he'd salvaged a pair of Letterman tickets I'd received three days earlier.

"Gracias," I said, and he took the envelope from me, pointed at my name and address on the front, and jotted:

FOR PROOF
OF

RESIDENCY.
(FOR
RED CROSS
HOUSING
ASSISTANCE.)
I WOULD
HAVE BROUGHT
YOUR PURSE BUT

He began a fresh page:

COULDN'T
FIND IT.

"I guess I'm not the most organized," I said, and he smiled, then coughed up phlegm and spit as he laughed, holding my shoulder to steady himself, or maybe to let me know that, yes, his vocal chords and part of his jaw were missing because he had cancer.

As it turned out, he'd *had* cancer. Of the larynx. And it had spread, so he'd had surgery twice to remove it. Or so Etta told me during a breakfast of cornbread muffins and America's Choice grape juice after I'd returned to the gym. And this news (which made me wish I'd hugged him when he and I parted ways on 49th Street), along with the reality that most everyone who'd come to that gym for help was at least twenty years older than me, sort of calmed me, or maybe just told me to take things more slowly, because I was almost as close in age to the old people around me as I was to the students who played in the gym—and the older you get, the more you need to learn to relax to stave off illness and death. Maybe, I thought, Ernest's cancer owed itself to the fast life he'd lived in his days as a Yankee, and I remembered an article in the *Times* about how, on the average, Manhattanites have heart attacks seven years earlier than

Floridians, and I recalled how I'd thought about dying when I'd given Ernest mouth-to-mouth, then wondered if my love affair with New York was really a well-appointed desire to live a fast, short life now that I'd failed in my relationship with Thom. This was unsettling, believe me. And it didn't help when it dawned on me that the difference between me and homeless people was essentially a father I rarely talked to and a few friends in Kankakee, some of whom had bet against me.

That's why, after Darcy showed up with her hair still wet from a shower and a presumably insufficient night's sleep, I shot up my arm after she requested a show of hands about who needed help finding a new place to live. This request would prove to be the closest thing Etta and I would get to an official announcement that the building had been declared uninhabitable, but I didn't know that then, and anyway I was startled by how Etta hadn't raised her hand. When I asked her why she hadn't, she told me that, if nothing else came up, she'd live with her sister in Brooklyn. Then Darcy explained two options for those of us who'd raised their hands: take a free room in a hotel while you looked for an apartment on your own, or ask to be part of a new program the city council had launched, which matched people who needed roommates with people who'd been burned out of their homes. A free hotel, I thought, would feel like a perk—until Darcy mentioned that the hotel was in The Bronx, and that the rooms would be free for three days only. Then, with her eyes zeroed in on mine, she mentioned that the program was designed to help people without significant others, and I told myself, Yes. That's for you.

Chapter 7

The city council's plan paid your first month's rent, as well as a thousand dollars to the person who agreed to take you in, and my new roommate's name was Sarah, and she lived on Grove Street, in that part of the Village where maze-like streets test your sense of direction. Sarah had oak-brown hair bobbed at this hip place on Astor, sunken blue eyes she'd raise every morning with more mascara than I'd used in high school, and a smudge of rosacea below her right eye, and the first thing she'd tell anyone we'd meet when we'd go out was that she'd been in this thing called "MFA-at-NYU"—that's how she always said it, "MFA-at-NYU," as if it were some kind of code that meant everyone who heard it should kneel at her feet. It's some kind of program where writers learn—well, I still don't know what they learn. From the get-go, my take on novels and such was that there's a lot more to the world than the tiny parts of it writers have stashed inside books. Plus: Since according to Sarah, you had to be a great writer to be accepted by MFA-at-NYU in the first place, why would you, if you *were* accepted, want to do anything other than write? I asked her this while we ate left-over pizza for breakfast the day after I'd moved in, and she explained, in a tone on the haughty side, how there was more to writing than writing, how you had to read the works of the great authors (and analyze them and discuss them), and how you needed a professor who'd written published books to show you "craft"—and these professor-writers had agents who might sit in on classes, *and* writers needed agents to get published.

But the hitch I noticed was that no professor of Sarah's had ever even mentioned an agent to her, or to any other student in her classes. Or so her former MFA-at-NYU friends said when they gathered at our apartment, which they did every week. Sarah called these gatherings "workshops," but to me they were more like half-baked parties. They tried to make it like it had been in their classrooms, where, at seven-thirty every Thursday night, someone was scheduled to bring copies of a chapter of an unfinished novel and read it out loud and everyone else was supposed to suggest ways to improve it, but half the time, when they tried to—as Sarah put it—"replicate this scenario" in our apartment, the writer scheduled to read a chapter would forget to bring it, and then this writer would leave to get it, and while she was gone, everyone else would get high and discuss how poorly she wrote, or how her work didn't reference novels of dead writers, or, if she weren't a woman but instead one of the two guys in the group, how he was a sexist pig. Which made absolutely *no* sense to me.

And when the writer actually did have the chapter there, she would stand and read it out loud in this extremely serious, snobbish, doomsday-worthy voice, which always made me wince because all of them used *the exact same tone.* Plus the writer could read only half a page before someone would interrupt to talk about a published book they were reading, and then everyone would start talking about published books *they* were reading, and then they'd all be dropping names of authors they'd read, three-word names like Charles Everett Graves, and they'd always ask the writer who'd brought the chapter if she'd read that author, and the writer would always say yes. But the writer would say this in a way in which I'd know it was a lie even though I was in my room with the door only an inch ajar, but what really killed me about this whole "Have you read so-and-so" game was that, if everyone there read every book they said they'd read, none of them could have written a word.

And they acted as if reading and writing were the only important human activities, as if someone who hardly read or wrote because she spent time outdoors growing wheat or something else *necessary for people to live* was somehow inferior. Think about it: If you're starved and don't have so much as a bread heel in your apartment, or if you're flirting with a stranger or making love or having a baby or watching someone die, who really cares about books?

Plus these people rarely got back to talking about the chapter they were there to improve, and if they did, they'd focus on one sentence for an hour and a half, taking turns calling it "fluffy" and "derivative," or trying to revise it without a writing utensil in sight, or arguing about, for example, the use of the word "and."

And if they couldn't think of something negative to say, all they would say was, "It works."

Once, after the last person finally left one those workshops, just before three in the morning, I asked Sarah if any of her friends had finished *drafting* a book, and she folded her arms and said, "Eric did."

Eric was a guy who tried to be cool by shaving his arms. Of the two men in the group he was the definite hetero, with to-die-for curls of shiny black hair and a beard trimmed like the one on Jesus, but he talked like a Valley chick even though he was from Grand Rapids, Michigan.

"He wrote it before he got in the program," Sarah said. She was shit-faced from wine. "Without feedback."

"Anyone else?" I asked, and right as I did, I realized she'd think I was asking about her.

"No. But novels take time, Michelle."

"Did it get published?" I asked.

"What."

"Eric's book."

"Not yet. He's looking for an agent who can help him revise."

"I thought your professors were supposed to do that."

"My professors were assholes."

And that ended *that* conversation.

Eric wasn't the only MFA-at-NYU alum who tried to be cool. There was Genevieve (which they pronounced "Zhawn-Veeyev"), who wore those expensive thick-black-framed glasses that actresses use to show how they can still look pretty despite them, only Genevieve wasn't pretty at all, though she did have a boyfriend who painted and put the same powder-blue Salvation Army sofa in the background of every canvas he finished. And she'd gone to Harvard for a year, which was probably why the rest of them let her talk longer than anyone before they'd interrupt to argue.

There was also Judith, who was pretty—she had the best skin I've ever seen on anyone, six-month-old babies included: you couldn't have found a pore on her if you held a magnifying glass an inch from either of her nose creases, which I'd still like to do. She also had naturally full lips that were heart-shaped without lip liner, and her teeth were so straight I'd always hope she'd talk so I could hear how precise she made consonants sound. Her neck and shoulders and arms and waist were remarkably thin, but her hips, when she got up from the chair she always sat on beside the fireplace that didn't work, were far too suddenly wide, so she wore these puffy tie-dyed pants that, if you ask me, looked like the kind circus clowns wear; in my mind, I called her Clown Butt. Which she deserved because she never said anything good about the chapters anyone else wrote, except for once, when Sarah read the first page of a novel about Prague she never finished.

There were also The Hat Triplets. I called them that because one was a Lynn and the other two were Lindas and I could never keep them straight, but also because they always wore hats, even when they sat in our apartment, as if hats were far more crucial attire than the bras they never wore. Sarah told me that one of them, one of the Lindas—the Linda who kept rewriting the same paragraph the entire time she was in MFA-at-NYU—had worn a hat in one of their classes toward the end of their last semester, and that everyone, including the professor, pretended not to notice the hat, but for the next class, the other two, Lynn and the other Linda, wore hats also—and, still, no one, not even to make a joke, even whispered the word "hat." Even though they had enormous brims, the kind you see on maids of honor at Midwestern weddings or women at the Kentucky Derby.

Then there was Syd, who might have been gay, but you couldn't say for sure, because he usually wore this LA Dodgers T-shirt and polyester thigh-hugging buttoned-back-pockets shorts, the kind gym coaches wore in high school, and because he was always flirting with Genevieve, though the way he'd flirt was that he'd kid her about her boyfriend the painter, asking her all sorts of questions about her boyfriend's paintings as if he, this Syd, had, as Tom used to say, "a hard-on for the guy." It didn't bother me that Syd might have been gay, just that he seemed too bent on trying to keep the rest of them guessing about his sexuality, as if he were constantly daring them to break down and ask. What confused me was that all of them seemed to consider him and themselves doubly hip because they knew he was daring them to ask but none of them ever would. I just never *got* that, especially when, supposedly, they all wanted to be writers and they weren't getting published. You know: Almost all their mental energy was being put into themselves and how the rest of the group thought of them, so how much could have been left for their books? Or, for that matter, for their relationships?

The only one who didn't try to be cool was Cecilia, the daughter of a famous writer whose name I can never remember. Sarah told me that, at the very beginning of the first class on the first day of her MFA-at-NYU, the professor (who no one in the room thought of as an asshole yet) went around the conference table asking everyone's names and where they were born, and Cecilia said "Cecilia" and her last name, which I'm sure I'll remember when I'm eighty-six years old, and that the professor, as a joke, said, "Believe it or not, folks, this is the niece of the man who's written more than a dozen bestsellers," and everyone laughed except Cecilia, who said, "Actually, I'm his daughter." I guess everyone got quiet then, including the professor, who, when he finally did talk, stuttered for five minutes about how to write the first line of a bestseller. Anyway, I liked Cecilia because she wore the same Levis and scuffed tan flats every time she showed at our apartment, even though she probably had gaga money from the millions of books her father had sold, and she always complimented everyone else's writing, and a third of her hair was gray but she never colored it. She didn't seem old enough to be gray, maybe twenty-eight, though when you're that wealthy you probably eat organic food for snacks so it's hard to tell your age, and the third that was gray wasn't distributed evenly—it was this nearly oval white patch that sometimes looked like a beret. In any case, I always found myself, when I'd walk out of my room for, say, a Granny Smith from the kitchen nook, glancing at her the way you do at someone you have a crush on, but you had to feel sorry for her because she never wrote anything.

Actually, I shouldn't say that. Once she wrote a poem, which she brought into the workshop on an impossibly rainy Thursday night, after lightening cracked just outside our building and Sarah got in a snit about power surges and turned off the lights and lit her sandalwood candles, which she'd stuck to her dead grandmother's Fiestaware and placed asymmetrically on the floor on the off chance she might bring a guy home. So the apartment felt tense when Cecilia read her poem, which she prefaced by saying it was the first piece of writing she'd finished in her life, and that she hoped it was, "in its own way"— her words—the outline of a novel. That made everything all the more tense, because everyone there had to be thinking that, if she could just finish this book, her father could get it published no problem, which was probably the only reason she'd gotten into MFA-at-NYU.

Then she read the poem, which took ten seconds tops, and it was about catching her father—who slept in a room down the hall from his new wife ever since he'd threatened to beat her with a tennis racket—trying on a pair of control-top pantyhose, and lightning struck the moment after Cecilia finished reading it, so everyone there had to be sure that all she needed to do was expand what she'd written into 200 or so pages—even I, spying through my barely open doorway, had goose bumps. I mean, it was obvious that her father would never help her get anything like that published, but on the other hand there had to be someone dying to print something as revealing as that.

What was odd was that none of the rest of them said anything to that effect. Instead, they ignored her and went about their usual business, Syd asking Genevieve about her boyfriend's newest painting, Judith enunciating extremely clearly while she tore into Ernest Hemingway with one of The Hat Triplets, who refused to touch her hat even though its brim covered both of her eyes, the other two Hat Triplets ignoring their hats with equal restraint as they discussed Rilke, Eric tilted back on Sarah's semi-antique chair with an I-wrote-a-whole-novel-but-it's-still-not-published look on his face and his hands folded over his crotch except for the moments, fifteen seconds apart, when he'd raise his index fingers to tuck his black hair behind his ears. Cecilia still had her poem on her lap, waiting politely, it seemed, for him or someone to look at her, but no one did, and I wanted to go out there and sit beside her and talk to her but didn't, because Sarah always frowned when I invaded her precious inner circle. Instead, I closed my door hard, hoping Cecilia would hear and realize that I'd made it a point to eavesdrop on what she'd read, and then I told myself she probably hadn't cared about the sound of my door at all.

But after everyone left and Sarah was washing her face, I found the poem lying on the couch, as if Cecilia had left it for me. I read it quickly to make sure I finished it before the faucet squeaked off, then again slowly, trying to memorize it, and I kept thinking about how I didn't know anything about poetry except that I liked what I liked when I liked it, and that here was a poem I cared enough about to want to keep—and that, if Cecilia knew I'd read it twice in a row, she might have felt better than she must have felt right then, which couldn't have been all that good. Then I told myself that I was thinking what everyone in that group but Cecilia thought—that my own opinion was so damned important— and Sarah, with the faucet still running, said, "What are you doing?"

"Cleaning," I said. "Someone left this here."

She beelined toward me, her hair held back by a terry cloth headband, then snatched away the poem, which she skimmed.

"Cecilia brought this tonight," she said. "A fucking *poem*. I'll have to give it back to her next time."

I picked up an ashtray and walked to the sink. "Do you like it?" I asked.

She skimmed it again, too carelessly to have read every word, then glanced my way and shrugged. "I don't know," she said. "I guess you could say it works."

She folded it and stuck it under her armpit, then walked to the bathroom and, with the faucet still running, lifted the toilet seat cover and sat down to pee.

"Goodnight," she called as she swung the bathroom door closed.

"Goodnight," I said, and I admitted to myself one of those truths that seemed better to ignore: Sarah and I would never be life-long friends.

Chapter 8

Cecilia never wrote after that, or if she did, she never brought what she'd written to the apartment, just sat on the same end of Sarah's couch under her white beret of hair and praised anyone who managed to bring a chapter to read, even though most of that stuff inspired yawns. Then, a few Thursdays later, she stopped showing up, and two weeks after that, no one in the group showed up at all. Except of course Sarah, who didn't wait past seven-thirty-five before she went jogging for the first time in her life. Only The Hat Triplets bothered to call with excuses: a new job, a vacation, and one of them was moving to Canada. I realized, when I couldn't sleep one night and thought about the disbanded workshop, that Cecilia was probably the only reason they'd spent their Thursday nights together in the first place; she, in the minds of the rest of them, was their last potential link to someone—her father—who might help them become famous and literary. And I figured that, after she'd read her poem, she'd kept enduring them because she'd hoped one of them might take the time to do what her father had never done—help her write more than six lines that barely made it halfway across a page—but after no one even looked at her as they'd continued to drop authors' names and brag about how many novels they'd read, they'd workshopped the last of her hope out of her. It unnerved me how everyone in that group had acted chummy while all they'd really done was pull the wings off the dream they'd shared on their first day in MFA-at-NYU, and at times it flat-out scared me. I mean, *Sarah* had been in that group.

This fear wasn't exactly squelched the morning I walked seven blocks to a wholesale produce market and happened upon Eric, the novelist who shaved his arms. He was leaving the market and lighting a cigarette when he noticed me, but he faced away from me as he fingered his black hair behind his ears.

"Eric," I said.

He glanced my way as if caught by surprise, his matted eyelashes proof that he'd been upset. "Sorry," he said. He dabbed the corner of an eye with the heel of his smoking hand. "I was having one of those...moments."

"Hey, I cry all the time," I said, though I couldn't remember the last time I had.

"I'm actually fine," he said. "It's just that—ah, you don't want to hear this."

"No. Go ahead."

"It's just that sometimes everything here feels a little too cutthroat. I mean, if I weren't such a dove compared to some of the people I've met here, maybe I wouldn't feel so overwhelmed."

He dragged on his cigarette, and I took one of mine from my purse, and he lit it. I inhaled hoping nicotine would calm me, which it did, but then my mouth went dry, and I felt a new tightness in the tops of my lungs.

"Sometimes I cry because I'm so happy," Eric said. "I mean, I can't believe we have so much potential. You know how many people wish they could be us? Living here, I mean?"

I shrugged.

"Everyone in the world," he said. "Or close to it. Sure, people in places like

Utah aren't all that into New York, but back in Grand Rapids, everyone I know wishes they were me. Which sounds egotistical, but I don't mean it that way. I just mean they wish they could have up and left and moved here like I did. None of them would admit that out loud, but you can tell, you know? You're from the Midwest, right?"

"Yeah."

"Chicago or something?"

"Kankakee."

"Then you know what I'm talking about."

"I think so."

"I mean, it's like if you're from the Midwest, you're, I don't know, expected to prove yourself."

"To people back home?"

"Actually I meant to people who are born and raised here."

"Like those people in your writing group?"

He forced smoke from the back of his throat, then nodded. "Not bad examples. And talk about cutthroat. Don't get me started."

"Are you saying Sarah's a cutthroat?"

"Not in those words."

"But you didn't really like her."

"I don't think anyone in that group liked her, even though we all acted like we did. It was as if she was always, I don't know, manipulating us. I hate to admit this, but she phoned me once and disguised her voice and pretended to be an agent who wanted to meet me about my novel. So I get all worked up, buy a new shirt and even a fucking *tie*, and go to this agent's office and walk in and say, 'I'm here for my three o'clock appointment.' And the receptionist says, 'I have no idea what you're talking about.'"

"That's terrible."

"Yeah. I told everyone back home that things were starting to happen, and now they won't stop asking about it."

"I can't believe Sarah would mess with you like that," I said, though part of me had to wonder.

"Neither could I. In fact, I first blamed myself. But before our last workshop, I told Syd about it, and he glanced over at Sarah, and she winked. I mean, why else would she wink? Plus, *someone* called me pretending to be that agent. Who else could it have been?"

"Still," I said. "You can't prove it."

"I know. And if I'd ask Sarah about it, she'd just deny it. So I'll just go on pretending it never happened."

"Maybe it didn't happen," I said. "Maybe it was just, I don't know, a clerical error?"

Eric dropped his cigarette and crushed it out with his steel-tipped boot. "I can see why you'd want to defend her. I mean, with her being your roommate and all. But I'm telling you, Michelle. She winked at Syd. And it was one of those sinister winks."

Chapter 9

From then on, whenever Sarah was home with me, I'd want to ask about the prank call on Eric and say she could have been nicer to Cecilia. But I knew that if I spoke my mind, she'd probably point out how I sometimes ashed on her floor and left bran flakes on bowls when I washed our dishes. Of course they were her bran flakes—I washed every dish she used—but to mention these facts would be asking for an argument, after which *true* deterioration could follow.

So I'd tell myself that, as a lover of Manhattan, I was lucky to room with Sarah, and that she wasn't really mean-spirited, just a seasoned New Yorker who'd taken a few lumps of her own. True, she'd banked good cash from the Red Cross for letting me live with her, fashioning herself, in that sense, a profiteer if not a cutthroat, but her example could teach me how to survive the city. And her style sometimes worked for me, especially when I haggled with tourists over the price of Letterman tickets. But then she began hanging around Walt.

Walt was a guy my former friends in Kankakee would have called a hands-down dork. I tend to go easy on dorks because I qualify as one: for example, I prefer clothes that cover my navel, and songs by Phil Collins can still make me cry. Anyway Walt was, in his words, "tweaking a dissertation on Chaucer," which doesn't guarantee dork status but sure provides a running start, and his head was shaped like one of those cock-eyed single peanut shells, his silk-thin red hair parted to cover baldness wherever it could. Sometimes he parted it to the left, which my Kankakee friends might have considered hip since, to them, going left with anything symbolized counterculture, but his pompous manner suggested he'd never protest a war, even despite his wire-rimmed bifocals.

Sarah met him at NYU, where he'd been delaying his Ph.D. in English for years while awaiting a tenure-track position at the University of South Dakota, which is, as he informed me, "nestled in a town called Vermillion"—where he'd been born—though he also said he would have taught in North Dakota, where his girlfriend since high school lived. I always wanted to tell him that there was no way this woman had stayed true to him throughout his years in Manhattan (that if he moved back to North Dakota, her real boyfriend would appear), but I didn't, probably for the same reason no one else did: even though you sensed he despised most of humanity, you felt sorry for him.

He did have lots of female friends, possibly because of this very pity factor. He was—dare I mention it?—walleyed, and he had harelip scars that turned blue in cold weather, both of these conditions the results of a birth defect that made him legally disadvantaged and therefore likely to get a teaching job in Vermillion because universities prefer to hire legally disadvantaged people over just about anyone (something I still don't believe but Sarah insisted was true, though she did say never to tell anyone I learned about it from *her*). My point is, Walt knew he'd be a professor someday, that it was only a matter of time before female students at the U. of South Dakota would throw themselves at him for A's, so he had bullish self-confidence. For a week after I met him, he never spoke to me, and after he finally did, he'd often lecture me, explaining more than once how "encyclopedia" means "circle of knowledge."

His attraction to Sarah, I figured, lay in his passion as a collector of female friends (were they his safety net because he knew his girlfriend was cheating?); I was sure Sarah hung with him because she needed a new shtick to hype her intelligence now that she'd quit writing. Around him, she drank green tea rather than her usual instant decaf, and she was always talking up his "theories," which extended beyond Chaucer and literature into the socio-political implications of how carpenter ants follow one another in lines. What got me most about Post-Workshop-Sarah, though, was that, with Walt now around, only she and he mattered. I mean, before Walt first appeared in the apartment, Sarah at least *seemed* to embrace the idea of groups of friends who could help one another, but after Walt showed up, her allegiances were with him only.

Sometimes I wondered who bothered me more, Walt or Sarah, but then I'd remember my father's advice when I'd been a kid: if people bug you, figure out what they have that's lacking within yourself. Whenever he'd yelled at me, I'd wanted to tell him to apply this nugget of wisdom to himself, but now, maybe out of latent respect for him due to loneliness, I took his advice and admitted that what Sarah and Walt had—and I lacked—was companionship.

The solution, of course, was to find a friend of my own. But I no longer met people as often I had in Kankakee, maybe because Manhattan *did* teem with cutthroats, maybe because I didn't go out as much as I used to, maybe because my job hawking Letterman tickets didn't lend itself to friendship. I was, after all, a sole proprietor, and after I'd make a sale, instinct still urged me to hightail it home. No, I wasn't running a shell game, but I never saw what happened to my customers when they showed up to see Dave. Were they admitted without question? Were the serial numbers checked to assure that whoever held a ticket had requested it by mail? Every *Late Show* fan knew Dave took security seriously, so I might have been selling worthless tickets. I didn't know I was, but I didn't want to know, and to exchange phone numbers with a customer would have been cavalier.

And without friends to humor me, I felt even more under duress when, a few weeks after Sarah steeped her first green tea with Walt, Letterman's mojo began to run thin. Or at least it had ebbed to the point that, after I left the apartment and cabbed uptown and stood beside the Ed Sullivan Theater with two tickets sent to me by a spinster cousin in Oak Park, all I could work was ten dollars each. And this disturbed me beyond my need to pay rent. I mean, it struck me that, in the days when my business had flourished, Dave had just returned from heart surgery, which suggested his fans had clamored to be near him when they'd feared he might die—but now that he seemed fit for the long run, few were willing to pay to see him. Which raised a point that made me queasy: Love is based on supply and demand?

If that were true, my scalping gig might fizzle. It's *not* supply and demand, I'd think as Walt and Sarah refined yet another Walt theory. The world loves Dave, and it always will. And trusting this belief, I did go out and sell four tickets for sixty dollars apiece. But on an autumn afternoon when I was moments from a deal with a French woman who wanted to see Monsieur Letterman and held out fifty-dollar bills as if they were tissues, an usher from Dave's lobby floated out toward me and said, "Ma'am, you can't sell those."

"I'm sorry?" I said.

"Those are complimentary," he said. "For you only."

And the French woman stuffed the fifties into her pocketbook, snapped it shut, and hailed a passing a cab that screeched to a stop to pick her up.

"I'm sure you're aware of the laws against scalping," the usher said.

"What are you talking about?" I said.

"What else would you call what you're doing?"

"I don't know," I said, and I turned and tried to hail a cab myself, blushing from my forehead to well below my neck. Cabs, I realized as I waved, might soon cost more than I could afford, and my breaths quickened faster than my thoughts. I'd had an easy cash-flow, but now the tickets in my hand might have been contraband. I felt stuck, right out there on Broadway, where three women a decade younger than me strolled past yapping about five-hundred-dollar-a-pair shoes. I was still without friends, and if only the damned usher would quit star-ing at me, I'd stop waving at no one and take the subway home.

Chapter 10

Thanks to an unabridged dictionary Walt kept on Sarah's kitchen table, I learned without a lecture from him that the third definition of the word scalp is "to buy and resell at significantly higher prices," and my own theory said that since I didn't buy the tickets I sold, I hadn't, technically speaking, scalped a thing. I had still, in my thirty-four years, never committed a crime; I could still soldier forth in my business without guilt.

Of course it was also still possible that Letterman's security people would have me arrested anyway, so I decided to operate on Broadway and 52nd, roughly a block from the Ed Sullivan Theater's marquis, where I'd watch to see who stopped to read the sign on Dave's front doors, the one that explained that tickets needed to be requested months in advance, then hit up whoever proceeded in my direction. This strategy worked, though success now required more time, and after Dave's fans reached me, they'd seem suspicious of my tickets, maybe because they wondered why I was selling them *there*. Or maybe it bothered them that, as I'd deliver my spiel, I'd check over my shoulder to make sure no one was watching—like the decked-out prostitutes who strutted past me, glanced at me, and glanced away.

In any case I no longer felt as high as I had the day I made my first sale. I still offered tickets to a show that attracted enthused audiences, but on most afternoons, whether or not strong demand met my supply, something in me was missing. It didn't help that, back at home, Walt was now around at least ten hours a day, which made me feel out of place—and confused me since he and Sarah never acted like a couple. Alone with her one morning, I asked if they'd ever made out, and she shook her head no, but from then on, she was, to use a Walt word, "inordinately" edgy around me.

And Walt now monopolized conversation with his theories and opinions, so Sarah and I barely communicated. We might chat while he used the phone, but either she listened to me or I listened to her, as if we were merely emptying the attics of our minds, both of us knowing that, if I ever said Walt bothered me, she could stomp into my room, point at all the clothes and empty wine bottles on the floor, and *castigate* me for being *slovenly*.

Then came the overcast October Monday I stood near 52nd holding out Letterman tickets as if they were as worthless as menus for yet another Chinese restaurant. I stayed there all morning and afternoon, and every potential customer cruised past. Dave began taping that day at 5:00, so by four, I was offering tickets for six dollars apiece. But no one bit. Not even for two. The lower I'd gone, the faster people had accelerated to put me behind them. At four-thirty, I felt like such a schmuck I thought: You're weeks away from Kankakee. Go see the show yourself.

So I got on line with the fans who'd sent for their own tickets, and they were so charged up I felt out of the loop. If their tickets had them this revved, why hadn't someone bought mine? Was I unaware of a hygiene issue? Had the time arrived to try rice cakes? Then I noticed that most of the people in that line were either nerds, spoiled college kids, or tourists, hardly any there on dates, many cracking jokes with Letterman intonation. Two undergrad guys in front of me studied the backs of their tickets, and one said, "You can't beat the price of admission," and they both laughed—and, for a moment right then, I almost *wanted* to leave Manhattan.

Then a guy in jeans and a navy blue T-shirt walked down the line handing out green sheets of paper. I thought *he* was pushing the menu of yet another Chinese restaurant, but I heard him say "tonight's taping" to someone in front, and it hit me that he worked for Dave, so I took one of the sheets, a photocopy of *Late Show* stationery headed with the words RELEASE FORM. One of the undergrads told the other that a woman ahead of them had said Dave was recruiting for Stupid Human Tricks, that all we had to do to have a chance to be nationally televised was jot down our tricks and names and addresses and signatures, and then everyone was borrowing pens and discussing what they'd say to Dave if they were picked. People were practicing stupendously desperate tricks, like hopping up and down on one foot while singing the national anthem, and I thought: I can do better than that. So I jotted down something I'd done moments before I'd met Thom —lodge a beer bottle in my cleavage and chug it through a straw. When the guy in the navy blue T-shirt returned to pick up the forms, he took mine, read it as he walked off, stopped in his tracks, turned with eyes still on my form, furrowed his brow, looked me up and down, and said, "You'd actually do that?"

"Why not?" I said.

And I meant it. Because my old friends in Kankakee might see me on TV with Dave: I was paving my way back to the Land of Lincoln.

Then the guy collected the rest of the forms and stood beneath the marquis reading all of them. He walked toward me, jerked his head to the side, and said, "Follow me," which I did. He said the same thing to six other people, and we, the fortunate seven, followed him past envious glares into the theater's lobby, through a gray hallway, and down carpeted stairs to the basement.

It was musty down there beneath a low ceiling of exposed pipes and wires, and an intern told us to "chill," which we did, except for a woman who practiced her birdcalls. Maybe nervousness had caused her mouth to go dry; she kept asking if any of us had seen a water fountain. Soon the guy in the navy blue T-shirt and jeans returned with a beer, a straw, and a pastrami sandwich, as well as more guys in dark T-shirts and jeans (Dave's writers, I figured, since each of them had a legal pad and pen), and he handed the bottle and straw to me and the sandwich to a bean pole of a man in a suit likely from J.C. Penny, then told the seven of us we needed to audition. "Dave has to know you can *do* these things," he explained, and the thin guy immediately raised three fingers, shoved the pastrami sandwich into his mouth, lowered the three fingers one at a time as he chewed, and opened his mouth to prove that, darn it, in three seconds, he'd swallowed a deli sandwich. Then the birdcall woman began chirping louder than the most grating of subway brakes, and a writer told her to stop, and the guy who'd brought down the beer nodded at me.

I have to be braless to get the bottle to fit, so I pulled off my bra without taking off my blouse, then twisted off the bottle cap and shoved the straw into the bottle, stuck the bottle between my boobs, and drank. After I held the bottle upside-down to prove it was empty, three of the candidates applauded, which shocked me because I'd figured all of them cutthroats. It was as if those three were so sure I'd get chosen they'd decided, What the hell, she deserves to flirt with Dave. A writer eyed me and asked, "Could you try that with a tallboy?" and everyone laughed, and another writer scrawled something, maybe that punch line, on his legal pad, and I realized that my nipples were hard, and I wondered if I'd been applauded for *that*.

Then the remaining candidates auditioned, two with food-consumption tricks without cachet and two with tricks they couldn't pull off, and a writer told those four to return outside, which they did, and all of Dave's entourage headed upstairs. The birdcall woman tried to shake one of their hands, but he ignored her. The thin guy sidled toward me and asked what I thought of Dave's website, and I said I'd never seen it, and, as if he believed he'd talked his way into my heart, he remained there, breathing through his mouth—a trait that never fails to turn my stomach. Then an usher appeared and said something to the birdcall woman, who followed him up the stairs. With a glance at the thin guy, I said, "I think we're supposed to go with them," and he shrugged, bumping my shoulder as we tried to catch up. At the top of the stairs, I saw the birdcall woman pass through a doorway, which I rushed through, and then I was there, in Dave's studio.

Contrary to television studio lore, it was bigger than it looks on TV, and the birdcall woman was following another usher down the aisle on the left-hand side of the studio, the side in front of the band. He seated her maybe halfway down, turned and assessed me and the thin guy, then walked toward the stage and waved us down, and a third of my way to him, I recognized him as the usher who'd caught me selling tickets. Not him, I thought as our eyes met, and he pointed at the aisle seat directly beneath the yet-Shafferless band, which struck up a Blues Traveler song, and the thin guy and I both froze, as if we were both too kind to try to beat each other to the seat, which any Letterman fan would kill for. The thin guy sneezed without covering his mouth, propelling me ahead for health reasons, and as I continued toward the seat, I looked to my left so the usher wouldn't recognize me, then sat and exchanged nods with the dreadlocked guitar player. After four drumbeats at most, the usher walked off to seat the thin guy, and I thought, Everything's fine.

But then the usher returned and stood directly beside me while actually twiddling his thumbs, which reminded me of my high school economics teacher and resurrected all manner of anti-authority feelings inside me. Finally, he tapped my shoulder. I sighed, then glanced up.

"You're that scalper, aren't you?" he asked.

"I don't think so," I said, and we engaged in the requisite stare-down—me bracing myself to apologize for every ticket I'd sold—until the band cranked up Chaka Kahn's "Once You Get Started" and he shook his head and walked off.

He'll squeal, I thought. And Dave will cancel your trick.

Then Paul came out, and the band went silent, and I folded my arms and tried to smile and remember if Dave normally showed two tricks or three. I was sure it was three, which would have made me indispensable, but the more the word *scalper* unhinged me, the more I believed it was two. Then I thought, Shouldn't I be backstage? Stupid Human Tricks happen *on* stage. I was positive they did, but then I wasn't certain of anything; like the birdcall woman, I was a wreck. I turned around to smile at her, but she was gone. As was the thin guy. It's them, I thought. Dave will air two tricks, hers and his.

Then the ticket holders from outside burst through the doorways at the rear of the studio and rushed down the aisles, and the band segued into Eric Clapton's "Why Does Love Got to Be So Sad?" Several of Dave's fans danced in their seats in asinine fashion, and I tried to lose myself in the music also, but I knew my trick had been cut, and as I sat through the taping I felt depressed, even with Dave there in the flesh.

What really got me, though, happened after the show, when the audience herded me toward the side doors onto 53rd Street: an intern cut in front of me and gave me a canned ham. "The show wants you to have this," she said. "If you avoid the theater from now on."

Had I thought quickly enough, I would have refused the ham and played clueless, but she rushed off and up the stairs to the stage, and the audience, in their post-brush-with-Dave glee, pushed me onto the sidewalk alongside 53rd, where two Letterman freaks closed in on me like magnets.

"You got a *ham?*" one of them asked, a man roughly my age with excessively bleached horse teeth and feathered blond hair. Maybe six other of Dave's fans pressed in on us. "Frank McManus of Astoria," he said, and he stiffened his hand so I could shake it, which I did, but only because my posse (as it were) sprouted a collective facial expression that said if I didn't, they'd consider me rude.

"What happened to your trick?" someone asked—the birdcall woman.

"I don't know," I said. "Politics?"

I'd intended that answer to imply that we all go home, but it glued eyes onto mine.

"It's always politics," the birdcall woman said. "Which is why I want you to have this." She opened her purse, pawed at its insides, and came up with what might have been her grandmother's cigarette case, which she pried open with a neon pink fingernail. Inside were neon green calling cards, and she gave me one: "Francine McManus, ACTRESS" over a 718 phone number and an address in Astoria, Queens.

Frank *and* Francine, I thought, and I thanked her for the card, since politeness seemed the best way to part with them quickly, but all it did was knot everyone closer to me, the presumed mother lode of connections to Letterman.

"We're into entertainment," Francine told me. "If you want to network or whatever, give us a call."

"We'll help you eat," Frank said, and he nodded at the ham, then wiggled his eyebrows.

"Seriously," Francine said. "Have you ever been to Astoria?"

That word—Astoria—was all it took to disperse the crowd around us. "No, I haven't," I told Francine, and it occurred to me that, to afford rent, I should walk home rather than take the subway, and then, as if something solid inside me cracked, I couldn't bear the prospect of walking home alone only to spend another evening avoiding Sarah and Walt. My armpits were sopped, my chest tight, my forehead hotter than it had been when I was nabbed selling tickets.

"Are you all right?" Frank asked.

"Sure," I said.

"You seem flustered," Francine said.

Here I'll admit that when strangers show insight into me, I sometimes disclose more, as if I want to be a victim of the kind of murder that earns its own logo on the six o'clock news. Thom had complained about this, believing I told strangers at parties more than I'd tell him, and I'd always called him paranoid for it, but now, as if to prove him right, I said to Francine, "I am a little upset."

"Wanna talk about it?" Frank asked, and he took Francine's hand, and the sight of them side by side, he of the monstrous teeth and Seventies' coif, she of the birdcalls and infatuation with neon, both of them shamelessly proud of each other and their residence in Astoria, sort of charmed me. These weren't sophisticates who might be cutthroats; these were enthused, down-to-earth human beings who, unlike Walt and Sarah, offered their friendship, and who was I to turn them down?

"I guess," I said. "I mean, if you guys want to listen."

"Of course we do," Frank said, and Francine nodded twice.

"Okay," I said. "I guess, when you get down to it, I have a roommate problem."

"Ah, the *room*mate," Francine said. "What's your name, anyway?"

"Michelle."

"Where do you live?"

"The Village."

"The Village is a home run," Frank said, and his eyebrows wiggled again, which on one hand made him twice the flirt he'd been on 53rd Street, though I reminded myself that repeatedly wiggled eyebrows on men tend to mean nothing at all.

"And let me guess," Francine said. "The roommate is male."

"Actually, no," I said. "But the problem does have to do with a man. He says he wants to live in South Dakota, but he and my roommate seem to be taking over the apartment."

"Ah, the squeeze-out," Francine said.

"Sorry?" I said.

"Roommate A and Roommate A's love interest squeeze Roommate B out of the apartment so Roommate A can mate without the presence of a third party."

"That's what I sometimes think," I said.

"Happens all the time," Frank said.

"But, see, they don't seem to be mating," I said.

"Then what are they doing?" Francine asked.

"Talking."

"*Talk*ing," she said.

"Yes."

"About what?" she asked.

"Mostly Chaucer. But also about ants. You know, whatever this professor-guy wants to talk about. And the problem is, they just *keep talking*, as well as ignoring me, and it starts to feel like I'm in the way."

"That's a squeeze-out all right," Frank said.

"You need to assert yourself," Francine said. "I assume you're paying rent there."

"Of course."

"So you have rights. You don't assert yourself every once in a while and they'll have you out on the street."

"I know," I said. "It's just that, right now, I can't see myself doing that."

"You need partners," Frank said, and he offered his forearm to Francine like the male lead in a musical set to promenade with a doe-eyed starlet, and she hooked her arm around his. Then he offered his other forearm to me, and he and Francine froze, and I realized they both believed I'd give him my arm and we'd all skip to the Village as if Broadway were the fucking Yellow Brick Road.

"I'll stick with my ham," I said, and they laughed more loudly than Letterman's best quip had deserved. And I hadn't been kidding, just trying to put my foot down about Frank's apparent self-concept: Frank of Irresistible Charm Among Women in Every Borough.

When they stopped laughing and caught their breaths, Francine said, "Seriously, Michelle. We're offering to come over tonight, eat your ham with you, or do whatever you think might help you assert more of a presence around these people. If you aren't comfortable with that, say the word and we're on the next train to Astoria."

"With absolutely no hard feelings," Frank said, and he wiggled his eyebrows, which bothered me, then made me laugh.

Chapter 11

As my fingers recognized the key to my building's security door, the old me wanted to punt the canned ham onto Grove Street and tell Francine and Frank to take it to Astoria and eat it themselves, but the new me, the one bolstered by their friendship, pressed on.

"This is a nice building," Frank said, and I opened the door.

"It has its faults," I said.

"This is awesome," Francine said.

We took the stairs up, and I readied my deadbolt key. You could hear Walt drone, I realized, through a fire door. Then I unlocked and opened that door and walked in, Sarah and Walt sitting on the couch in their discussion mode: cross-legged and hunchbacked and facing each other directly. After Walt finished his latest dependent clause, Sarah paid me a begrudged glance, and I said, "Sarah and Walt, I'd like you to meet the McManuses."

"Oh," Walt said glibly.

"Of Astoria," Frank said, and he thrust out his arm like a duelist and headed straight for the couch, where Walt stood, hands at sides—until Frank grabbed one, shook it, and said, "Walter, right?"

"That's correct."

"That's one helluva shaving cut," Frank said, and he pointed at Walt's harelip scars, and Sarah shot me a look that said *I* was responsible for the outside world when it came to the protection of Walt's ego.

Walt himself shrugged and blushed. "Nasty," Frank said, and he grabbed Sarah's hand and said hello and pumped the limpness out of her arm despite her frown, and right then, with the apartment at its upper boundary of silence—no human voices inside or out, no traffic noise, not even the scuffling of a cockroach—I would have forked over a decent chunk of my dwindled savings to hear *anyone's* theory. Because this silence implied anger that would mount into lectures I'd hear (probably from Sarah) about how audacious I'd been to contaminate the Village by importing a jerk from Astoria. And I'd be lying if I didn't add that, during most of this silence, I felt almost sheer sorrow for Walt—since it occurred to me that, someplace in his impressively analytical mind, he'd likely divided his experience into the times when people had mentioned his harelip scars and when they hadn't because they'd preferred to ignore him.

Which shows how mushy I am. I mean, I couldn't dislike Walt for three seconds after his mammoth ego had probably only been nicked. True, I'd brought over Frank and Francine as a sort of revolution against Walt's tyranny, but now I felt as if I'd dropped a second bomb on the Hiroshima that was Walt, the first being his harelip itself.

Finally he muttered "Pardon," and he straightened his wire-rims with a thumb and headed for the bathroom in the poised manner of a real professor. After he shut the door and we all heard it lock and raised our eyes from the fake Persian rug that covered all but precisely six inches on each side of Sarah's floor, my eyes first, Frank and Francine's next (simultaneously), and then, finally, Sarah's, Francine said, "Hey, let's fry up that ham."

"Did you say 'ham'?" Sarah asked with a scowl.

"In fact, I did," Francine said. "You got a problem with that?"

Usually when two people I've introduced seem headed for conflict, I try to make peace as soon as possible because I played social coordinator in the first place, but in this case I needed to choose between the Frank/Walt harelip scars controversy and the Francine/Sarah ham controversy, and, under that duress, my heart went out to Walt. So while Francine and Sara exchanged unpleasantries, I set the ham on the floor and eased backwards out of the living room, then walked down the hall toward the sound of the faucet running behind the closed bathroom door. To try to ignore Sarah's anti-ham rant (which, no doubt, was rooted in her recent conversion to veganhood owing to Walt's online article about Upton Sinclair), I gazed at the fire escape framed by the window at the end of the hall. Then the bathroom faucet squeaked off, and I imagined Walt studying the mirror image of his harelip remains for the 12,000th time in his life, and feeling a sort of love for him, I knocked on the bathroom door.

"Sarah?" he said.

"It's Michelle," I said. The door opened maybe four inches, telling me, I figured, that he wanted us to talk through the space, but I pushed the door open with one of those gestures you make and regret before it's done but keep doing. His glasses were off and scissored between two fingers, his left nostril plugged with a twisted section of Sarah's unscented toilet paper, and he was blotting his face with the folded hand towel she'd set out in April, his wet hair parted violently to the left, a splotch of blood under the tip of his chin.

"Nosebleed," he said, pointing to the nostril. "From stress. Rest assured I haven't shed any tears."

"I believe you," I said, though I didn't believe him completely. "I just want you to know I didn't think Frank would say what he said. In fact, I'd kind of forgotten about your..." I waved vaguely toward his face. "Scars."

I reached for the hand towel, which he let me take.

"And this might sound...sophomoric," I said as I wiped the blood from his chin. "But I think we should try to be friends."

"That'll never happen," he said, but I was already moving in to kiss his cheek, my eyes barely open when his face squirmed like a shy cat's, so I made contact just beneath the plugged nostril, smack on the harelip scars that had begun the whole ordeal. I remained silent so he could respond with words, but he slid on his wire-rims, yanked the toilet paper from his nose, tossed it at Sarah's Ecuadorian wastebasket, missed, contorted himself to get past me, and walked off.

I decided to let the toilet paper lie. Why bother? Wasn't I headed for Kankakee? After all, Walt was obviously still on a warpath because of the shaving cut comment, and there was still the issue of the ham, both of those concerns having buried my need to assert myself. I returned to the living room, where Frank, Francine, Sarah, and Walt stood stiffly in a nearly perfect semicircle, as if they'd just discussed the wine bottles in my room and decided I needed an intervention right then and there.

"How are we all doing?" I said.

"Sarah prefers that we eat the ham in Astoria," Frank said. "And apparently this apartment is more hers than yours, so we want to do her a solid and respect that."

"A solid?" I said.

"I believe that means a favor," Walt said.

"So?" Francine asked me. "Would you like to come with us?"

"I don't think so," I said. "Go ahead. And take the ham. I kind of lost my appetite."

"Okay," Frank said, and he hoisted the ham off the floor. "How about lunch at our place tomorrow? This is ten pounds' worth, you know." He raised his eyebrows and kept them up.

"I have your number," I said, and I nodded at Francine. "Sorry this didn't..."

"*Work?*" Sarah said, and Frank and Francine walked to the door, where they struggled with the deadbolts, each attempt to unlock all of them resulting in at least one remaining intact.

Finally they were gone, and Walt crossed his arms. Sarah glared at me as if she were my mother and I were sixteen and pregnant.

"I hope you felt that was worth it," she said.

"Worth what?" I asked.

"Upsetting me."

Those two words echoed as if they'd both begun and ended an argument, which convinced me that I'd win any forthcoming argument; it was only a matter of convincing *her* of that. So I went straight for the jugular: "Let's not get melodramatic here, Sarah. No one, not even a life-long vegan, gets emotionally bruised at the sight of meat—" I swallowed from pre-victory nervousness. "In a can."

"I'm not talking about meat," she said. "I'm talking about Walt."

"Sarah, I cannot control what Frank or anyone says. And if I want to bring friends home, I think—"

"She's not talking about Frank," Walt said. "She's talking about your little move."

"What move," I said.

"Michelle, let's not get duplicitous," Sarah said. "Walt told me about your pass in the bathroom."

"My what?"

"Your sexual advance," Walt said.

"What sexual advance."

Walt lowered his chin to study me through the correct halves of his bifocals. "Did you not kiss me?"

"Yes, but that was just a gesture—"

"It was a kiss."

"But I told you I wanted to be friends."

"That's what they all say," Walt said, and Sarah stiffened and cleared her throat.

"Even if I fucked him," I asked her, "what do you care?"

She smirked at Walt, and he smiled back, and, without turning toward me, she said, "I'm his girlfriend."

"And I'm supposed to *know* this?" I asked.

"You should have assumed."

"So—what—you broke up with the woman in South Dakota?" I asked Walt.

"North Dakota," he said. "And I haven't broken up. But I will."

"And you believe him?" I asked Sarah.

"Yes," she said. "Michelle, maybe you haven't noticed, but Walt and I are... advanced. If he were in Europe and his ex-girlfriend were his wife, no one would care if I'd sleep with him."

"But *you* care that I kissed him. When I didn't even know you and he were... intimate. In fact, Sarah, I asked you if you were dating him. And you said no."

In front of the building, a bus groaned past.

"You asked if we were making out," Sarah said.

"And?"

"We don't *make* out," Walt said.

"Right. You guys skip foreplay and just hop to it."

"Maybe we do," Sarah said. "And maybe that's none of your business."

"Well," I said, "I'm glad it's not."

Which was one of those things you blurt because you're so beside yourself you can't think of anything else—and then you feel so belittled by what you've blurted, you either huff off or face ridicule. So I huffed off, to my room. Actually I walked very naturally the last two thirds of the way and left the door open so they wouldn't have the satisfaction of hearing me slam it, but then I was in there, trying to convince myself that my nights in that precious space weren't numbered in the lower single-digits, and grabbing my clothes off the floor and cradling what I'd grabbed since I neither knew where my luggage was nor wanted to make a production of trying to find it. Because if they saw me find it, one of them might ask if I were returning to Kankakee. And if I answered in light of what Manhattan had taught me about supply and demand and people, my answer would have to be yes.

Chapter 12

My forearm numbed by the weight of gathered clothes, I sat on my bed (or, actually, Sarah's bed) to fold each item as neatly as possible—and decide if I wanted to stay in Manhattan, and if so, what I could do about it. Memories of Thom assured me that I did want to stay, but I didn't want to argue with Sarah and Walt, since they were *patently* better armed than I when it came to wars of words. And even if I'd win a final argument about my rights to keep my room, the prize would be re-runs of The Walt Show, which hadn't at all been what I'd wanted when I'd left Kankakee.

An apartment of my own would have solved everything, but that would require money and luck, neither of which were exactly flowing my way. It would also likely require a recommendation from Sarah, as would attempts to room with a stranger in Manhattan. What I needed, I realized, was a *person*: someone who lived in Manhattan and cared enough to vouch for me if not simply solve the problem of where I should go. Del, of course, was out of the question, and Etta, as kind as she'd been, presumably still lived with her sister in Brooklyn. She's all I got, I thought, and I swallowed away the last of my hope. I'd never believed in a god with a capital *g*, but I was now poised to appeal to an other-worldly spirit, maybe not a traditional, throne-perched god but maybe a more amorphous one, like a karmic vapor that might help desperate saps such as me.

That's when I remembered Ernest Coolridge. And that he'd been Etta's *super*. Whether he still worked as one was questionable now that Etta's building was vacant, but I smiled at how he'd befriended me without saying a word.

I glanced beyond the stacked clothes on either side of me for Sarah's cordless, but it wasn't on my bed. Nor was it on the floor. I strode out to the living room, where Walt and Sarah, flopped lazily on the couch, ended a whispered tiff between them. I looked around the room, and Sarah's eyes followed mine as if she were waiting for me to speak, which of course wouldn't happen. I felt like Ernest Coolridge himself, silenced but unashamed. Finally I saw the cordless on the mantel of the useless fireplace, and as I snatched it I realized that Ernest's speechlessness meant he might not *have* a phone. But Joyce could field his calls, I thought. Dialing directory assistance on my way to my room, I remembered something Joyce had said: Ernest Coolridge wasn't his actual name. Dammit, I thought. Why didn't you ask him who he was?

Just inside my room, I clicked off the phone. I reached for the door to close it, then heard Sarah say, "Michelle?"

I turned and faced her, empowered by my silence. The longer I didn't speak, the less she would say to hurt me. I was a child again, and this time it felt good.

"Walt and I were talking," she said. "And—"

"We want to offer a compromise," Walt said.

Out of his mouth, the word compromise scared me. I kept my eyes on Sarah and said, "And?"

"I'm willing to pay back the rest of this month's rent," she said.

I shrugged.

"And give you half of the money I got from the Red Cross," she added.

I nodded and stepped further into my room.

"Does that mean you agree?" she called.

Over my shoulder, I said, "No."

"Then what did it mean?" Walt asked.

"That I'll think about it."

And think I did after I closed the door. What *they'd* meant, I knew, was that Walt had now displaced me altogether. Maybe he wouldn't use the bed I'd dreamt on—maybe my room would be his office—but their point had been that I no longer lived where I stood. I was on my own, thrown out, whatever Sarah and Walt and I wanted to call it. Yes, I could contact a renters' rights group with the phone in my hand, but if that group intervened on my behalf, I could kiss goodbye Sarah's offer to buy out the dubious rights I had. And as much as silence had empowered me, my leverage could fade if I didn't say I'd take her cash soon. And other than eight hundred dollars crammed into the toe of a red leather boot in my closet, all I had were folded fives and ones in various sections of my wallet. Karmic vapor? I thought. If you exist, tell me what to do.

As if to taunt me, the phone rang. I was afraid I might cry if I answered it, so I returned to the living room, where I handed the cordless to Sarah.

"Why don't you answer it?" she asked.

"Because it's yours," I whispered.

She switched it on and held it to her ear, and I walked off and heard her say, "This is Sarah," her version of Walt's first words into any phone, and then she was right behind me, tapping my shoulder, and she said, "It's for you."

Again, I turned. Again, I sought privacy in the room that was no longer mine. "Hello?" I said as I closed the door.

"Michelle, it's Francine."

"Hey, Francine."

"Frank and I were about to get on the N, but we wanted to see if you were all right."

"I'm—wait, how did you get my number?"

"Frank read Sarah's name off her mailbox. And I called directory assistance? I hope you don't mind."

"No. I guess not. I mean, it doesn't really matter."

"You sound upset."

"I am."

"We figured as much. So we just thought we'd re-invite you for dinner. Again, no pressure. Just say the word and we'll get out of your hair."

"I appreciate the offer, Francine, but dinner's the least of my worries."

"What do you mean?"

"You really don't want to know."

"Oh, but I do, Michelle. Frankie's saying we just missed the train. Go ahead. I'm here for you. Take a deep breath, then let it all pour out."

Chapter 13

Whenever it comes to moving, I get serious and sad and philosophical. Serious because a move is up to you to accomplish by yourself (no one I've known has ever even been *around* to help); sad because when you pack, you find dried flowers and matchbooks and other miscellany you'd paste into a scrapbook if you were the scrapbooking type; philosophical because moves mark the passage of time in your life more deeply still than birthdays, since moves mean another large portion of your life has ended, which brings into question how many portions of any size you have left.

So I don't want to dwell on my move from the Village, other than to say that my lack of a New York driver's license meant I couldn't rent a car in Manhattan, and that my numerous boxed possessions required me to pay for three cab rides to Astoria, and that while I did this, Frank and Francine, if I were to believe them, were off in their car hunting for tag sales in the nether regions of Queens.

Francine, true to her word, had left a key to their duplex under the only

white rock in their yard, which of course meant that they'd preferred to risk bur-
glary by a neighbor who'd seen her hide the key to having to help me lug boxes,
and that, after I set down my last box in their living room, I was again alone.

I grew curious about the guest room. For an entire five minutes, I sat on
their IKEA couch resolved not to snoop, but then I said, "Go ahead and snoop"—
those words actually left my mouth—and as I stood I instructed myself to proceed with self-control.

I found a bathroom, a wartime supply of rhubarb preserves in a linen closet,
then a room with a twin bed, an IKEA night stand, and an armoire crowned by
my canned ham. Then I happened upon their bedroom, but as soon as I saw it, I
heard keys jingle outside their back door—and I dashed on tiptoes to the couch,
where, as Frank walked in and saw me, I plopped myself down and crossed my
arms and legs.

Neither he nor I (nor Francine, who was directly behind him) let on that
I'd been caught. Instead, Frank hugged me long enough to tick off your average
wife, but Francine, apparently nonplused, hugged me just as long. Finally they
said hello, Francine as she squeezed my fingertips, Frank as his eyes held mine
like an outer-borough hypnotist. I have to say that, as greeters, they knew how
to make a person feel pretty damned uncomfortable.

"So," Frank said, and we studied their parquet floor.

"You look great, Michelle," Francine said. "Let's show you your room."

"That would be lovely," I said, and I let her lead me, and Frank followed me
with his hands on my shoulders, which I twitched to give him the (ineffective)
message to let go. When Francine reached the guest room door, I realized I'd left
it open, but she glided past it and extended her arm with a theatrical flourish.

Frank steered me onto the mauve carpet, finally let go of my shoulders, and
said, "Huh?"

I balked in search of an answer. "Beautiful," I finally said.

"You think?" he asked, and I nodded despite residual discomfort from his
hug, and he said, "Beautiful room for a beautiful woman," and, certain Francine

would put the kibosh on his flirtation, I shot her a soured expression only to see her eyebrows rise.

"I have to tell you guys how grateful I am," I said. "I mean, I really owe you, so the last thing I want to do is overstay my welcome. So tomorrow—first thing?—I'm off to find my own place."

"In Astoria?" Frank asked.

"Where else?" I said, and I realized something that I now believe everyone's gut has presumed since humankind was in the primate stage: you do what you do because you have to. Sure, there's that pop-psych maxim that says people *choose* to do things ("you make *choices* with *consequences* for which *you* and *only* you are *responsible*"), but let's face it: I didn't exactly choose to leave the Village for Astoria, and I sure didn't choose to ingratiate myself to a couple that, looking back on it, seemed off-kilter from moment one—I freaking *had* to. I realize that the idea is that a woman in my shoes could have chosen to return to Kankakee right then, but had I done that, I wouldn't have been a woman, since, to me, womanhood begins with dignity, and running back to Kankakee would have brought me lower than dirt. After all, had I returned to Kankakee then, my father and my friends and Thom would have feigned respect for my time in New York while all of us *knew* they considered me a loser for having failed so quickly.

Anyway Francine was pulling down the orange corduroy bedspread, and as she fluffed the pillow, she muttered, "Take Frankie with you."

"To *bed*?" I said as a joke, and she and Frank each released a breath of laughter.

Then Francine said, "That's up to Frankie" in that quick, quiet way people blurt earth-shattering statements that leave you wondering if you heard wrong.

"You know of some empty apartments, Frank?" I asked, to smooth it over either way.

"Absolutely," he said. "We could do it wherever."

And all of those words had come out clearly: I had no doubt he'd said them, and as if to underscore them, he grabbed the sides of my arms and turned me around to face him, then held my chin with his fingertips and kissed me on the lips. It was one of those quick, closed-mouth kisses that at first seem innocent enough, the kiss a decent father might give a daughter after she pays for dinner, but after he did it, he didn't say anything, just remained so close I felt his breath against mine, and I heard springs in the mattress creak (from Francine sitting on it?), and Frank's eyes grew intent: both he and Francine, I was sure, were letting me know they were into sex with more than just them, in this case, with yours truly.

And I don't know what you're supposed to do when a couple wants to have sex with you, but what I did was turn my back to Frank (which didn't exactly help my cause—not to mention Francine was now *lying* on the bed) and play along with the innocent half of their double entendre: "An empty apartment would be great," I said. "I could move in right away."

"Or you could sleep here," Francine said, patting the mattress. "Whichever." She folded her arms and shifted her eyes from mine to her toes, which made me aware she'd slipped out of her shoes, then threw all of us into silence. I wondered if, during the silence we'd shared in the Village, they'd considered how I might look naked, and I got stuck on my own thought about how, if I ever *did* have sex with a married couple, it could never involve orange corduroy.

"We'll go first thing in the morning, Michelle," Frank said. "We'll get you a nice-sized studio."

And just like that, we were all pretty much back to the supposedly innocent way we'd been, because Francine asked me, "Thai for dinner?" and I said "Sure!" and she hoisted herself off the bed and stepped into her shoes and took Frank's hand as she led him out of the room and closed the door.

The way she'd closed it, though—completely, without asking if I wanted it closed—told me that, as she'd left, she felt angry, dashed, or hurt. Plus they'd held hands, which I assumed meant they were trying to show me that, even though they shared orgasms with third parties, they still loved each other. Or maybe they were trying to show each other that. And maybe the whole clingy-husband-and-wife routine was all about convincing themselves they were happy together even though they got off on kind of cheating on each other. It was all very confusing, which is why I'd deflected their offer in the first place: I still couldn't understand the romantic appeal of the couples-friendly-totally-nude strip club. All I knew was that the average McManus guest did more than sleep in their guest room, and that I wanted to leave their apartment and never come back. And that for as long as I'd lived in the Village, no one I'd met there had even mentioned the concept of a threesome, but that I could have been part of one   without even trying—within my first two hours in Queens.

Chapter 14

Perhaps needless to say, our Thai dinner was not the best of my life. An aftertaste of tension lingered from the impasse in the guest room, but I also kept thinking about how Frank and Francine were trying to be Manhattanesque by eating Thai when Thai was already ho-hum in Manhattan. Don't get me wrong. I love Thai. It's just that I don't beam with pride because a tangle of fried noodles sits in front of me.

And Frank and Francine *were* proud. Frank kept calling his Poa Pia a "home run," and Francine wouldn't stop about the dumplings. I wanted to talk about why I hadn't had sex with them, so I could explain how I didn't care what they did with their genitals as long as it didn't involve mine, and I just knew that, the longer we went without discussing it, the harder it would be to bring up. I mean, you don't just interrupt a conversation with a couple a week after they've made a move on you to say, "About that threesome you guys wanted to have last week"—because you just know they'd say "*Three*some?" with incredulous looks on their faces, accuse you of being paranoid, then go around telling people you know in common about how you like to walk on the wild side. I mean, I imagine that, among swingers, there's like a forty-eight hour cap on how long you have to discuss what happened or didn't, and then you're expected to go back above ground and pretend you're as normal as everyone else pretends to be. Or maybe you're expected *never* to talk about the subject of group sex before, during, or after, just "let it happen," then slip into a no-tell-pact that promises to make everyone involved feel liberated.

I didn't know. Which is why the Thai wasn't so hot. Then, after the Thai, we "*had* to have," as Francine put it, spumoni ice cream, which I never did like and nearly hated now that I was in this spacious but creepy duplex apartment in Astoria, because it seemed that Frank and Francine considered it the *Astoria* thing to eat for dessert, which would have been fine if Astoria were Paris—which it obviously wasn't since, as we ate the spumoni, a loudmouthed friend "called up" from the sidewalk through an open living room window, and Frank ran off to dangle his torso over the windowsill. Frank shouted his end of their conversation so loudly I heard every pronouncement of what he deemed as "aces," a "home run," or a "pisser."

I'm still not sure what "pisser" means. I think it's something that's both great and startling, sort of a home run with edge. Anyway while Frank and his pal were broadcasting their exchange and Francine and I were finishing our spumoni as if we weren't listening, I wondered if the pal had spent time with The-Frank-and-Francine-Tandem in the guest room bed that awaited me, and, if so, precisely who did what with whom, and all of a sudden my spumoni became a blob my spoon could barely dent. To finish it for the sake of politeness—Francine had finished hers, so the pressure was on—I concentrated on how wise I was not to express interest in the pal, since that might have suggested a *foursome*.

The word wisdom, then, was the silent mantra that helped me get down that spumoni, because, when I repeated it to myself mentally, it put my declination of

Frank and Francine's offer to, I don't know, give head to Frank while Francine gave it to me, in a fairly good light. I mean, no woman in her thirties sets out on an average day to be wise (it's embarrassing enough to be sensible), but after you turn down a *ménage à trois* and get over how you're sure the people you've turned down think you're a big virgin, you realize what some people who dive into multi-partner intercourse learn after it's too late: that sex with one person might never again feel as exciting, and that you can take the total number of people you just exchanged fluids with, subtract one (representing yourself), and use the remainder to multiply your general chances of contracting a *disease*. Especially if at least one participant had been imprisoned for heroin possession, which, given what Frank was now shouting, his pal actually had.

Then we had coffee, which was far more agreeable than the spumoni and somewhat better than the Thai—until Frank returned and I could no longer deny that he and Francine were sit-and-sippers: people who make coffee the heart of a ritual for being sociable at the end of a day rather than what it truly is, liquid caffeine. This might be stretching it, but I think one could call the coffee they served a "pisser." Because it tasted great, but while we enjoyed that taste, there was an edge to the air, at least to the air I was breathing. Because the more Frank and Francine sipped, the more they talked yet acted relaxed, which induced me, in order to display gratitude for my forthcoming night in their guest room, to talk and act relaxed myself—even though I still felt nervous because their relaxation seemed laced with hope that, now that they'd planted the idea of swinging into my mind, I'd say I felt warm, unbutton my blouse, sit on Frank's lap, and ask Francine for a spoonful of spumoni we all could share.

Then I did feel warm, which seemed unnatural since a breeze kept charging through their open living room window, though not unnatural in the miraculous way I'd felt the previous evening (when everything had fallen into place, as it were, to prevent my return to Kankakee), more in that foreboding way that makes you wonder if Satan and hell and so forth actually exist. To be honest, my body grew warm so suddenly I wished I *could* unbutton my blouse, and I couldn't help but imagine a Lucifer-type angel who'd just quit the ranks of my friend the karmic vapor to work as a double-agent for an anti-vapor aimed at tricking unaroused people into having kinky sex. I'm not saying kinky is evil, just that I wasn't up for even your basic two-person missionary right then, and that this warmth felt like a supernatural force undermining my preference to keep my clothes on. But I was armed with suspicion that Frank and Francine were still working angles, and I kept myself buttoned, and Frank and Francine continued to sip and talk.

Then my forehead began sweating, quite the fine detail when you're "at rest" in a breezy room with relative strangers, especially after *beads* form and you grab a napkin dotted with Thai errors to wipe your forehead as if you're attending to face-shine under the threat that a *bulging drop* will fall from your eyebrow while you answer a question asked by one of the relative strangers. Please, good vapor, I thought. Cool me off. Then I found it difficult to breathe, which I blamed on the chain-smoking I'd done on those cab rides between the Village and Astoria, so I didn't much mind. But after a few dozen breaths it was still difficult, and then it grew worse than it had in years, bad enough to resurrect fear of a childhood enemy: asthma. I hadn't had a serious attack since the eighties and still carried an old inhaler in my purse, so I figured I wouldn't die, but even a low-grade attack right then would have rendered me suicidal, because if anything makes you a misfit, it's clinging to a scuffed inhaler with your eyes bugged out as you desperately and repeatedly *depress* the inhaler to urge it to work after its years of semi-retirement.

"Excuse me," I said, right as Frank began to explain how *he'd* been arrested for heroin but falsely accused, and I used my napkin on the corners of my mouth, blotted my forehead, then stood, pushed back my chair as peacefully as I could, and marched from the table into the living room. The breeze was stronger in there, which began to solve the perspiration problem, but I couldn't breathe for shit. Plus: I couldn't find my purse. Normally I keep it as close to me as soldiers keep rifles, but after hauling in all of those loads of my belongings and wanting

to snoop before Frank and Francine returned, I'd let myself slide on purse loca-
tion. Or maybe I'd known it but now forgot because of the thinning supply of oxygen to my brain. And if there's one thing that puts it to me, it's losing my purse,
because when that happens, you can't deny that your life is wildly off course.

In any case, the wheezing began, as well as what I knew to expect—the
scraping of chair legs against linoleum in the kitchen—and then Frank and
Francine stood in the doorway between the kitchen and the living room, apparently curious about the wheezing but too shocked to step over the threshold, no
doubt because my face was between scarlet and purple.

Francine managed to say "Michelle?"—and I gave her the okay sign, which
I knew looked insane but was actually more than wise because anxiety only
worsens an attack, and if they began asking if they should call 911 on top of my
well-suppressed panic, things could grow far more dire.

Then I managed to croak "Purse," which of course made more sense to me
than it did to them, but it proved I could talk and thus calmed them enough to
prevent Frank from giving me the Heimlich as an excuse to feel my boobs.

In fact, all I could think of just then was how long he'd hugged me when
they'd first come home, and how their desire to seduce me might have been because she'd told him my nipples had gotten hard when I'd auditioned that ridiculous trick for Letterman's writers while she'd waited to do her bird calls.
"Did she say...purse?" she asked now, and I nodded. Then, with possibly all of
the breath available to me for the next thirty seconds, I went for it with an entire
sentence:

"I need it."

"You need your *purse!*" Frank shouted, and I responded with three exaggerated nods, and then I was throwing the belongings I'd moved from the Village all over their living room, including the baseball mitt my unmarried aunt
had given me when I'd been ten, a cigarette carton full of matchbooks I'd stolen
from clubs, and the jar I'd kept pennies in after I'd thought an ingrown armpit
hair was breast cancer and realized I didn't have health insurance, but my purse

was nowhere, and my last three spoken syllables—"I need it"—had taxed my pulmonary system into more than a bind. And it's bad enough to be unable to breathe, but when you know your own personal stages of breathlessness and approach the stage wherein the sum total of your knowledge won't help you (the passing-out-only-to-die stage), you feel drowned by thoughts such as *No, not in Astoria*, or *Not around swingers*; I mean, you hardly care about death and what you could do if you lived even a day longer—instead you're shocked by your circumstances now that your life will finally end.

Which can be a wake-up call about how you should probably move *again* if your friend the karmic vapor grants you another breath. And when your search for your purse has you throwing around belongings you never use, you almost, in such a situation, want to tell that vapor, "If I'm destined to move to where someone else does me a 'solid,' keep my next breath for yourself."

Which might sound desperate, but I wouldn't call it that. Because after Francine dashed into the guest room and returned with my purse, I felt pretty enthused. I still needed to unzip the purse and dig out the inhaler, which meant throwing all kinds of smaller but still embarrassing junk onto the parquet floor (my emergency pair of panties, the balding rabbit's foot Tom gave me that I'd totally forgotten I had, and seemingly hundreds of Boston Baked Beans I'd bought by the pound at a Midtown Rite Aid when I'd been starved one night only to forego after I saw an all-night Ray's a block away), but the familiar sensation of my fingers around the two worn leather handles of my purse assured me that, if I could keep my eyes from popping entirely out of their sockets for another eight to ten seconds, I might live. Then, on the very bottom of my purse, in the corner closest to me, beneath some crumpled but unused tissue and beside the Army surplus pepper spray dispenser my father had sent after I'd sold The Reliant, I felt the inhaler, and I pulled out both it and the pepper spray lest I mistake one for the other, studied them to make sure I didn't inhale pepper spray, tossed the pepper spray dispenser across the room so carelessly Frank had to duck, shook the inhaler six times, opened my mouth, aimed the mouthpiece past my lips, and began depressing. Only a hint of mist came out, which does spice your panic with regret about how you hadn't refilled the prescription the *last* time it barely worked, but I trusted my relationship with this inhaler enough to buy time with a smidgeon of oxygen from another wheeze, then shook the inhaler as if it were a can of spray paint for an overdue middle school art project, and essentially sucked on the mouthpiece as I depressed eight quick consecutive times.

Nothing came out, so I depressed like a madwoman—and it worked. To be fair, I should mention that, a millisecond before it worked, I hoped my friend the karmic vapor would enter the inhaler and order it to work, a hope which, given the inhaler's vaporous ingredients, could either lead someone like Walt to theorize about why, on the day before I'd moved to Astoria, I'd imagined The Supreme Being as *being* a vapor—or nearly confirm, in the mind of a cynic with at least the tiniest bit of faith, that the unlikely rejuvenation of my inhaler was a miracle thanks to the karmic vapor itself. Which I guess is my way of saying that, having gone through the ten minutes between when I began sweating for no apparent reason in Frank and Francine's kitchen and when I finally began breathing normally in their living room, I will, until the day I *do* die, always think of myself as a cynic with at least the tiniest bit of faith.

In what, I'm not sure. But that wasn't the issue now that I was back on oxygen. Now I had to smooth things over with Frank and Francine, avoid any leftover sexual desire of theirs aimed at me (which, unless they were into asphyxiation, didn't threaten to be difficult), and get through the night in their guest room without being disgusted into sleeplessness if the sheets weren't fresh.

"Sorry," I said. "I should have mentioned the asthma. If it's okay with you guys, I think I'll just turn in."

"Abso*lutely*," Francine said. "I'll set out some towels in the bathroom. And if you get hungry in the middle of the night, remember: everything we eat is communal."

"Thanks," I said, and Frank didn't wiggle his eyebrows, just reminded me we'd look for an apartment for me first thing in the morning, which I took to mean Francine's eating comment was free of double-meaning, and I noticed that my baseball mitt had landed in their fireplace, and a new wave of embarrass- ment struck. So I said, "Thanks for the Thai—the spumoni was really great," then wished them goodnight and headed for the guest room, where I left the door open an inch to imply I wasn't self-conscious.

But then, of course, I faced the awkward point that crops up when you're a guest in a one-bathroom place and the festivities are over and you don't know whether you should proceed with your bedtime hygiene ritual or defer to your hosts so they can go first since, darn it, the place is theirs. Usually I decide what's prudent by dawdling in the guest room to eavesdrop: if my hosts start to wash dishes or, say, step outside to smoke, I might slink into the bathroom and take care of business without having to see them and say goodnight all over again; if they head for the bathroom, I gauge the audibility of their activities, then decide—*before* I take my turn—whether I'll run the faucet full blast while I urinate.

But as I eavesdropped this time, I heard nothing, not even footsteps across their parquet floor. It was almost as if they'd frozen in the living room or tiptoed into the kitchen to sit-and-sip without clinking their spoons. After at least fifteen minutes, I still hadn't heard anything, and then their silence had lasted so long you had to assume they were asleep even though they'd provided no audible evi- dence of movement from where I'd last seen them to their bed, not even a telltale creak of their mattress. Maybe they shushed each other, I thought, and forewent brushing their teeth.

This theory, I was well-aware, risked possible interaction with them, but since I can't sleep unless I've scrubbed my face past my hairline and chin twice, it would simply have to do, and I took a healthy breath and left the guest room. The living room was empty, lit only by a small lamp, and their bedroom door was shut, and all of the other lights were off except a night light shaped like an elf that helped me see the open bathroom door. As I walked through the living room, I noticed, thanks to moonlight, that they'd taken the belongings I'd strewn and stacked them into a pile, the largest item a blue rain slicker (as they say in Kankakee) I'd never worn folded into a perfect rectangle on the very bottom, then increasingly smaller items topped off by a paperback I'd bought but never opened about how to be your own best friend. How they'd done this without me hearing a sound is something I still don't know, and after I'd made it into the bathroom and saw the set of Plaza Hotel towels stacked in the same manner, all I could think to explain their silence was that, despite everything we all knew about how odd we were, they'd decided to end my first day there by being nothing but polite.

So when I dozed into sleep between the guest room's fresh sheets, I almost considered living with them. But the next morning the entire apartment was still quiet, which, along with the gun-metal-gray clouds I saw through the guest room window, unsettled me into wanting to find my own apartment without Frank's help, and I dressed as quietly as I could, pulled my rain slicker from the bottom of the pile, grabbed my purse, and booked out of there. I had no idea what time it was, an ignorance that alone can make me feel out of sorts. I wandered to 30th Avenue, where failure seemed imminent for every storefront business, including several furniture outlets crammed with black leatherette sofas, black lacquer waterbed headboards, and those clash-prone floral print armchairs grandparents have: until I'd seen those stores, I'd never imagined you could buy chairs like that *new*. As a result, and despite the promise a new day can bring, Astoria struck me as the stop of last resort for goods that had crossed the Atlantic but had no chance in Manhattan, as if the import-export honchos on the west side of the city below 42nd Street just knew, when they saw a rack of polyester evening gowns from Romania, that they shouldn't let a dockworker bring them ashore, just order them onto a tugboat bound for Astoria.

It was depressing, I'll tell you, and knowing my goal was to live there by dusk made it all the more pathetic. As I waited out a DON'T WALK sign, I considered getting on the N and riding it to Brooklyn to try to rent a place there, but I'd been to Brooklyn, and it had struck me as roughly the same except a shout or two more harsh. And now, as I crossed the street, I realized that immigrants and scrappy white people were walking toward the N in pilled cotton-blend clothes that told the world they slaved nine to five in Midtown high rises but that, no matter their devotion, they'd never get paid enough to afford the city. That's when I decided that, if I did find a place of my own in Astoria, I'd draw the cris-crossed fire escapes framed by the window at the end of the hall in Sarah's apartment. Because if I could get those fire escapes down so they'd convey the peace I'd found in them, I might (I hoped) be considered as hip as the best artists in the Village, and maybe someday someone would buy what I'd drawn, and I'd use the proceeds to draw those same fire escapes from a new angle. And if I could get *that* angle down, I might try another, and if those drawings sold, I might believe there were thousands of hip angles left, and at some point, if I sold enough, I might be able to quit the job I'd needed to take in Astoria to pay rent, then use some of my money to move back to Manhattan.

This compulsion to draw propelled me up 30th Avenue and onto Steinway Boulevard, which Francine, while we'd eaten the spumoni, had talked up as if it were the Madison Avenue of Queens. From what I could see, Steinway Boulevard simply offered more of those irksome storefronts, though it did have a Gap and a pet store with dachshunds behind its windows—adolescent puppies making hay of shredded newsprint—and a shop that sold futons, and, more crucial, a real estate agent's office with yellow and pink 4 x 6 cards in its window describing apartments for rent. Those cards stopped me in my tracks and even, I'll admit, shocked me, not only because I needed my own apartment and there it very well was, but mostly because my time in Manhattan had put me in a frame of mind in which *any* unoccupied living space in New York was the Holy freaking Grail.

Plus: these places were cheap. At least relatively speaking. I mean, they weren't Kankakee-cheap, but one studio was going for $650 a month. Actually that place was in the basement of some Greek guy's house (he'd made it a point to mention he was "of lineage from Thebes") with no separate entrance, which

meant you'd likely have to walk past his baklava or whatnot if you brought someone home from a club. Then this mug appeared behind the window, belonging to
a guy taping up more 4 x 6 cards. Normally I don't use the word mug to refer to a
face, but in this case it's the only way to do justice to what this man's genes had
bestowed. His eyes drooped at the corners, and his lips were a sharp slant, and
his nose reminded me of one you'd see on a two-bit gangster in a Woody Allen
film. And he himself must have thought of it as a mug, because, even though we
were inches apart, he pretended not to notice me, which had to mean he felt self-
conscious, because here I was, a decent-looking woman obviously mesmerized
by the apartments on his cheerfully colored cards, which should have meant to
him that, either financially or sexually, I meant business.

So I gave him a break by backing off a few steps, and I noticed, in my reflec-
tion in the window, that my hair was sticking out in a high number of directions
(and not at all stylishly), an undeniable proclamation that I'd just up and left a
bed and didn't care if I looked like yesterday's oatmeal. No, my looks didn't let
on that I'd left that bed to escape a married couple who'd come on to me before
I'd slept, but I was flustered enough by the sight of myself that *I* pretended not
to notice *him* as I turned and faced Steinway's traffic to smooth my hair down
repeatedly, then repeatedly hard. Finally I walked into his office, and he said,
"Ma'am," and from then on, nothing that had happened at his window seemed
to matter, since he was my apartment-finding "friend."

Because almost every other sentence he used either began or ended with
that word. He'd say, "Let me open this book of listings, friend," or "Friend, did
you want a studio or a one-bedroom?" or "Here's one that just came in yesterday, friend." Now and then he'd also work it into the middle of a sentence, for
example after I'd explained that all I had to my name was $1,800 and he'd de-
scribed a $700-a-month "one bedroom studio in a pre-war building" that still
needed paint on one ceiling and polyurethane on its floor, and he said, "I'll tell
you what, friend: you won't find a better place for that kind of money unless you
go to New Jersey."

At which point I realized that, as odd as he looked, he was a slickster. So I asked, "What do you mean, 'one bedroom studio'?"

"It's got a bedroom. But it's also kind of a studio."

"And which war do we mean when we say 'pre-war'?"

"You know what, friend? I'm not even sure. Maybe Viet Nam?"

"Can I see the place first?"

"Friend, *there* we have a problem. Because I'm the only one here today. Not to mention the apartment is month-to-month, so if you don't take it, I'll guarantee you the next person who walks in here will take it unseen. I'm telling you, friend, it's that good of a deal. In fact you give me fourteen hundred for the first month and security, I'll call the manager there and talk her into waiving the upfront last month's rent."

"She'd do that?"

"She and I go back a long way," he said.

Meaning you slept with her, I thought.

"That leaves you $400 to fill your refrigerator," he said. "And buy your shower curtain."

And art supplies, I thought, though I couldn't shake my suspicion that, one way or the other, if I gave him the fourteen hundred, I'd be scammed.

"It's not the Taj Mahal," he said, a concession that both made him seem honest (enough) and hooked me into the whole I-want-to-draw-so-I-should-do-without mentality. Then he said, "But unlike that place for six-fifty, where you'd need nineteen-fifty up front, it would be all yours," and he opened the top drawer of his desk, rummaged through dirty rubber bands, pulled out a key ring with two keys on it, and tossed it onto his desk.

"How do I know those aren't just any old keys?" I asked.

"Look at me," he said, and he pointed to his nose, which hung down almost as far as his permanently angled lips. "And be honest with yourself. With a face like this, would I lie to you?"

Chapter 15

I was raised to believe the American Dream meant splendid reward for hard work, but let's face it: in this country the gist of everyone's nine-to-five is to bamboozle one's fellow citizens out of as much money as possible. Take for instance how bags of vending machine pretzels have grown not only more expensive but also smaller by such tiny fractions of ounces that no one but me when I'm starved, it seems, has noticed. Or how everything in Manhattan, after you've lived there awhile, obviously shortchanges people, like the three-card monte games that disappear as police approach, and the hotdog stands that seem fun until you read about how the vendors don't change the water your hotdog *lives* in until it's tweezed onto your bun, or the restaurants that charge the sky for meals that leave you hungry—as rats infest their kitchens like people in airports that handle so many flights a jet destroys a tower because a CIA hotshot ignored men who took flying lessons to learn only how to take off. My point is, go ahead and take advantage of me, but to then try to convince me that I'm cross-stitched if I don't trust easily is pushing, as it were, the envelope.

That's why, after I'd handed over most of my cash and retraced Steinway to meet the pre-war building's manager, I was confused by my trust of Mr. Mug. Even more befuddling, my trust seemed to grow the farther I walked from him. *Was* this because his face was hopelessly asymmetric? Or because he'd said my place wouldn't be the Taj Mahal?

Then I was on 38th Street, and I saw my supposed building, a five-story orange brick complex that had four different addresses and commanded two-thirds of the block, a kind of cousin of the projects you'd see in the Bronx plopped onto a street in Queens, and I trusted Mr. Mug all the more, which now exhilarated me. Looking back on it, I must have been so jazzed about having my own place I swallowed my fear about exchanging my cash for those keys—because I'd never lived by myself anywhere, not when I was a kid in a house with my father; not in college when I had roommates in dorms; not when, after college, I moved in with Thom and we'd endured a series of apartments in Kankakee thinking we'd marry; not with Etta in Midtown; not with Sarah in the Village; not for my curious stint with Frank and Francine. I guess you could say that, as I approached that orange building, I didn't trust because I'd been coaxed by reason. I trusted because, if I wanted to live alone in New York, trust was my only option.

I'm not saying I was completely antisocial that morning, just that I was on an independence kick. This might have owed itself to my need to recharge the social batteries after Frank and Francine's unconsummated overture, but I think it was more so because I truly wanted to draw those fire escapes and believed I couldn't without solitude. I'd tried to draw now and then in my thirty-four years, but either my father or some friend or Thom had shown up and complimented me in a way that sapped my fizz. You know: people who've said they love you see you doing something off the path like drawing or playing an instrument (once I bought a guitar and taught myself a thirteen-note stretch of Mark Knopfler), and this new you throws them for a loop, so they compliment you in a hollow way that makes you wonder if you're wasting your time.

Anyway I found a management office on the building's first floor, and inside was a giant (and I don't mean tall) woman whose knees etched a note in my mind not to eat any of the Greek pastries I'd seen on 30th Avenue, and she said Mr. Mug had said "good things" about me, which relieved me of the fear that I'd paid most of my savings for nothing. She grabbed two form leases from a stack on the floor and took me to the apartment: two rooms, one with the entire kitchen on one wall, the other a bedroom with a closet that had been converted into what had to be the narrowest bathroom in Queens. The walls of the place were all right, but the ceilings were crusty, though she said she'd have them painted the next day, so I signed the leases, and she took one and wished me good luck and left.

Then I re-read what I'd signed and saw that I was committed for twelve months rather than the month-to-month Mr. Mug had promised, and I broke out in a sweat because I'd been taken again: as much as I'd wanted my own place, a year in Astoria felt too much like a prison term, especially since, now that I was finally alone in a place that was mine and no one else's, it became all at once obvious that the ceilings had crusted because they leaked, a reality punctuated by the fact that, as I sized up a water stain, a drop fell into my eye. After I ran to the bathroom mindful of the wisdom to flush foreign objects from the human eye immediately, I learned that the bathroom faucet neither dripped nor ran. The kitchen faucet, I learned after I ran *there*, was fine. My eye felt out of danger soon enough, only to help me notice that the manager had signed the wrong line on my version of our lease, which could mean that nothing legal prevented her from evicting me on the spot, though given how things were coming along, that hardly felt like the end of the world.

Because what counted most was art supplies. I had to get some. I also had to move my belongings from Frank and Francine's duplex, but of course I'd just moved all that crap the day before, so I felt an inertia on its behalf, which could have been my own laziness—or ambition if I considered moving belongings as second priority to getting my drawing career on track. And I don't know if anyone cares, but I decided right then that it was fine to use "art" in the phrase "art supplies," but that I should always use "drawing" otherwise, because if there were one thing I couldn't take when I'd lived in the Village, it was people who'd used the expression "my art." Not to mention the crush of performance *artists* in the Village who, let's face it, can't make it as actors or comedians so they try to do both at once, only to bug the patience out of anyone who lacks the wit to leave before such a performance begins. I'd also met a guy twice in a club just off Avenue B who, both times I met him, said his pottery (which he kept photos of in his wallet and looked like a kindergarten ceramics project) was "art," and that his "talent" to make it was a "gift." Once he'd even said, "I've got the gift; I don't know where it comes from," and I'd thought he was poking fun at the numerous posers around us, but he was serious. My point is: anyone who draws or paints or acts or does anything well out of bounds from the All-American Job (typing, selling insurance, or otherwise staring at a monitor) should avoid the kind of self-praise that makes people struggle not to laugh.

Nothing, I decided, is art until someone offers to pay for it. And I wanted to get my supplies immediately, if for no other reason than my overall dearth of trust suggested I might never draw a thing, not to mention my apartment felt as if the mediocrity of Astoria had been concentrated into its 450 square feet. So I left, locking my deadbolt even though I had nothing behind it to lose. As soon as I'd locked it, I turned and saw a woman who lived directly across the hall unlocking hers, and I sensed she noticed me out of the corner of her eye, which in Manhattan would have meant she'd ignore me, but she spun around, stuck out her hand, and said, "Sandy. I guess we'll be neighbors."

Shaking hands with her reminded me of the handshakes Frank and Francine had milked when I'd met them after the Letterman taping, but Sandy proved to be quite unlike them, because, while she did seem to carry the Burden of the Insecurity of Everyone Who Lives in Astoria, she did it far more straightforwardly than they, yet somehow almost shyly; as she and I *got to know each other*, she kept squeezing her doorknob as if she wanted to escape me, but also talked on about herself as if I were her only friend. Her hair was coppery red, and she was thin but not from exercise, and she wore frumpy clothes and felt shoes and had the kind of general paleness (not restricted to her face) that suggested she hadn't been outside much in a quarter of a century, and besides those twenty-five years, her age was anyone's guess: she could have been thirty or fifty. She told me she worked as a "claims fairness oversight officer" for some state bureaucracy, and she went on about that, but I didn't care enough about government then to try to understand exactly what she did. I think she made sure car accident victims got back what they deserved, which meant her nine-to-five was aimed at making sure people *didn't* get bamboozled, but even though she worked against insurance companies, she still dealt with insurance, so I didn't consider her kindred enough to tell her that, for as long as I could, I'd spend my time drawing fire escapes.

Still, she was nice, and, as I mentioned, very straightforward. After three minutes tops, she said I looked like a cross between Meg Ryan and Kathy Bates, which is about as close to perfect honesty anyone can muster to say you're cute but could lose fifteen pounds, one of those facts about me I always have in the back of my mind but try to ignore. She'd also been a psychotherapist (before her claims fairness oversight gig), and she went to town about that, telling me about maybe six of her clients, including a retired construction worker who was hooked on antidepressants because, when he'd been single, he'd been too hung over to make sure a girder of a skyscraper in Manhattan was perfectly level, then later in life had all these nightmares about this skyscraper tipping and crashing into his daughter's apartment two blocks away; a twenty-six-year-old adopted Korean woman who'd grown up in Marin County and pledged celibacy (because her parents, who were hippies, had performed acrobatic sex acts in front of her), then left California to give Shiatsu massages in Manhattan for twice the money and didn't want to be a prostitute but gave guys hand jobs since, somewhere along the line, she'd become a sex addict; a geriatric transsexual who'd been a man before she'd had the sex change—but then wanted *another* sex change because men control everything. I kept wanting to ask her (Sandy) if some kind of law forbade her from telling people like me the details of her clients' problems, but I didn't because she seemed so honest I hated to throw tacks in front of her tires.

She also listened well, and I don't just mean with repeated nods and utterances of "yes" and "uh-huh"; she actually made you feel as if she cared about you, and I'm not sure how she did this. Maybe it had to do with how, when you broached something generally too personal to tell someone you'd just met, she'd divert her eyes to take the pressure off. Altogether she qualified so well to be a friend for life I couldn't help but remember (as I told her about Sarah's choice to live with Walt) how, on my first night away at college, my roommate Tess and I had lain in our parallel beds and talked so long I was sure *we'd* be friends for life, but a week into the semester, after I'd met rowdier students and this Tess met what she called "folks in campus ministry," we hardly talked at all until the end of the semester, when she requested a new roommate and I felt so estranged I didn't feel hurt.

Anyway I told Sandy not only about how I'd kissed Walt (which Sandy couldn't believe I did, even after I explained I'd done it before I was sure that Sarah wanted to live with him), and then, just after we laughed about how I'd probably take a month to call my father about my new address, her face grew sort of plastic, and she asked, "Michelle, why are you angry?"

Which is a question that always strikes me as misdirected, because everyone who claims to know about how "healthy" people are supposed to feel always tells you anger is the worst thing to have in your heart, whereas, if you ask me, there are at least two things that are far worse than anger: hatred and how you get stuck when you feel nothing at all.

Compared to those two things, anger, to me, is a picnic. Anyway my answer to Sandy was, "Who said I'm angry?"

"No one," she said. "It's just that you're so cynical."

"Then I'm cynical," I said, my stock response to that observation about me, and she didn't answer, which might have meant she was backsliding into therapy mode. In any case I wanted to explain to her that cynicism is more about happiness than it is about anger—because cynics are nothing if not saps who burn to be happy—but I didn't, because my desire to draw was spiking.

"That's cool," she said, which didn't sound like her.

"Hey, I gotta get...breakfast and stuff," I said.

"Don't let me stop you," she said. "Knock on my door whenever. We'll share a bottle of Chianti."

"Sounds good," I said, and those words came out so naturally I almost believed we'd actually *sit in her apartment and drink Chianti*, though I knew that was well off the unlikeliness scale, because, for one, Chianti, if I'm not mistaken, was big in the seventies, which told me she was probably past her mid-forties and therefore her candor would eventually grate, and, two, I wasn't up for drinking that day and didn't imagine I would be until I'd finished at least one drawing I wouldn't trash. Then we said good-bye, and she stepped inside her apartment as I began down my newest flight of stairs, and it killed me how many times in my thirty-four years I'd gotten along with people but kept cruising toward being alone.

When I got outside, Astoria didn't seem as dire as it had an hour earlier. It appeared more expansive, and I hardly felt bothered when, six doors ahead of me, a guy walking a pit bull let the thing sniff a tire on a parked Town Car, chomp on it, then clamp down so hard that, by the time I reached the tire, it was flat.

Something to draw, I told myself, and I continued toward Steinway Boulevard, where an art supply store seemed as likely as me ever living in Manhattan again, but where I was sure that, if it came down to it, the owner of some dusty drugstore would sell me a school-supply notebook and a pack of those no-nonsense ballpoint pens, the kind that seem to have less ink in them every time you trust pens enough to buy one.

Chapter 16

I found magic markers, the kind that don't make you high on their fumes but also don't bleed through paper to betray amateur status, as well as an actual drawing pad. I found them at a 99 Cents Store where, to economize, I also bought five off-brand colas and as many seriously off-brand boxes of sourdough pretzels so that, for approximately thirteen dollars (those places should be called 99 Cents-Plus-Tax Stores), I could ingest caffeine without the financial burden of cappuccino, as well as eat pretzels if I got on a drawing roll and didn't want to leave to eat. Then I stopped off at a bodega, bought a carton of cigarettes, went home, lit up, dropped the pad on the middle of the main room's parquet floor, knelt in front of it, sat on my ankles, and drew. This required that I support my torso with my left hand, which kept my cigarette just close enough, and I convinced myself not to expect the results of the first day to be all that hot, but part of me hoped the lines on the first page would *mirror* those fire escapes visible from Sarah's window, so after the first two lines defied the word parallel, I sat up and glared at them and smoked. Then I opened a bottle of cola, damning myself because the 99 Cents Store had stocked huge plastic drinking cups for *forty*-nine cents and I hadn't thought to buy one due to excitement about the drawing pad, and I swigged straight from the bottle, a move I found disgusting but would tolerate until I returned to the 99 Cents Store, which I didn't want to do. Return there, that is. It wasn't that I didn't like the 99 Cents Store (in fact, I'd kind of enjoyed it); it was just that I knew that, if I stopped drawing to shop for as much as a cup, I'd buy the cup, then wander down Steinway to the Gap and waste precious cash re-joining the average Americans who spend time shopping as an excuse not to do something as horrifying as teaching yourself to draw.

This decision to swig from the two-liter might seem insignificant, but it wasn't, because after I lit another cigarette and alternated swigs and drags until the bottle was a third empty and the apartment was full of smoke, I felt the atmosphere I'd need to draw parallel lines, and to complete them without freezing halfway and leaving that little mark.

Then I flipped to page two—but didn't draw. And I realized my cash reserves (or the scarcity thereof) might have explained why my lines weren't parallel: I was nervous because my inner clock was ticking toward the day I'd need a job for rent, and if that day arrived and I hadn't drawn anything solid, the job I'd get might absorb the time and nerve I'd need to draw long enough to have my results matter. The whole situation felt beyond a Catch-22, because I needed time to improve but also needed to beat the clock before I needed to work in order to afford the apartment—where I needed to take my time.

Relax, I thought, and I stood, crushed out my cigarette in the kitchen-wall sink, lit another, dragged on it twice, balanced it on the rusted edge of the stainless steel basin (ash-end in), shook my right hand to relax at least *it*, then forced myself to address page two. This time all I did was make uninterrupted lines, one after another, without thinking about parallelism or how often I'd gazed at those fire escapes when I'd roomed with Sarah, thinking only about how I was attacking the problem of the little mark, and now my lines ran so long most flew off the pad and landed as streaks on the floor, which hardly mattered because, if they didn't wash off, the place was a dump anyway. After maybe fifty lines at unplanned angles, I had the problem of the little mark licked, and page two looked infinitely unlike any pair of fire escapes—but was better than page one. I wouldn't say it was worth keeping, but it seemed less fearful, not exactly nervy, but a step, or maybe two, toward nervy.

Or so you think, I thought.

Then I let my hand do page after page of whatever it wanted, letting it curve what I'd thought might be straight, letting it wave instead of zigzag, allowing ovals instead of squares, and it wasn't until page seventeen that I acknowledged hunger and opened a box of pretzels and ate three and finished my first bottle of cola and reviewed. On four of the pages, I'd drawn nothing but curves and imperfect ovals, and, if you used your imagination, you could isolate sections that looked like eyes. Not to mention that, if any page were a keeper, it was among those four. Then I remembered that, at the 99 Cents Store, I'd seen a stack of watercolor sets, the kind in those black metal cases you shut with a muted snap, and I wondered if dabbing paint in the eyes to make them look more (or less?) human was merely a dodge of my inability to render even a single fire escape, or only my body's way of reminding me that my eye still felt scotched from the drop that fell into it.

Then I thought: What do you *want* to do? If I switched to watercolor eyes, I might have wasted the time I'd spent working toward magic marker fire escapes, which could have been a signature to put in all my drawings (like the powder-blue sofa Genevieve's boyfriend had worked into all of his paintings), or at least a step toward entire landscapes of Manhattan, not typical skylines or stretches of well-known streets such as Central Park West, but the cooped-up fire escapes and fences you see in the semi-private spaces behind buildings. There was something about those spaces I adored, probably how they never made it onto postcards tourists bought and sent home.

Still, the eyes were winning. Because they'd come out well. Or relatively well. Eyes, I thought. I'm into them. Why this meant my eyes needed to be painted was something I didn't think through until I'd left my building and bought a set of watercolors at the 99 Cents Store and returned and ran the kitchen faucet to moisten the skinny brush that appeared used despite how the perfect ovals of colors seemed untouched. Even after I thought it through, the only reason I'd conjured was *because I wanted to*, which, I imagined, had been the rationale of the guy in the Village who made that god-awful pottery.

But he's a poser, I told myself. Whereas you live in Astoria. And I touched the yellow oval with moistened bristles, mixed that much yellow with green, and made the white of my first eye something close to chartreuse.

Then I tore out the seventeen pages and set them in rows on the floor along the non-kitchen walls and painted one after another. As I painted, I tried to be thoughtful, and though my results failed to convey mastery, on certain eyes I had a decent thing going with yellow and green, as well as with blue and black. For a while, I wondered if it were too obvious that yellow, green, blue, and black meant fear, envy, sadness, and death. What got me most, though, was that red had been my favorite color when I'd been a kid but now stayed untouched in its oval.

Then I noticed it was dark outside, which meant I'd spent as many as ten hours painting, possibly more, because this darkness seemed more settled than the one I'd noticed when I looked out Frank and Francine's guest room window before I'd slept the night before, and I realized that, from their point of view, I'd been rude not to call them all day to say I'd found my own place and therefore wouldn't need their hospitality, thank you very much.

So I told myself to go out and find a payphone, but just after I unbolted my door and reached for the doorknob, it hit me that I'd left their number, along with my belongings, at their duplex itself, which meant I should probably at least walk there to "check in," but I didn't want to see them just then. I convinced myself it would be more rude to knock on their door if it were past eleven than it had been not to call them all day, though a niggling inside insisted it *wasn't* past eleven, though I couldn't bank on that since I didn't have a clock, and I began to like not having one. For a moment or two, I wondered if I'd drawn and painted all day to avoid Frank and Francine's libidos, as well as to avoid having to move my possessions from their place to mine, but if those were the reasons, there were worse reasons to draw and paint. The main thing had been that I'd worked as long as I had: if I'd ever be skilled enough to show anyone something I'd done, I had catching up to do. There were impulses, and there were results, and there was the need to know which of both to trust and which to abandon.

Then I decided that, when I would see Frank and Francine, I'd try not to tell them my new address, because now that I had a place of my own, I didn't want to see them again ever, other than to get my stuff. Which meant I'd used them out of desperation for a place to stay, which had arisen because Sarah had kicked me out of her apartment (which had happened, I finally admitted to myself, because I'd kissed Walt even though intuition told me she loved him), but then again Frank and Francine *had* tried to sleep with *me*, and I pictured my stuff piled in their living room and considered one question: What if you just never go back there?

Screw your stuff, I thought.

And I re-locked my door and returned to my work. Which, I'll also admit, sounds irresponsible, but I now had more than enough responsibility, since I was focused on my seventeen paintings, or, to be more precise, the next seventeen or seventy (or more) I'd need to begin and finish before anything worthwhile came of what a woman like me could do with a cheap paintbrush, four signature colors, and a decision to live with nerve.

Chapter 17

Everyone who's tried to do something like paint without the support of a wealthy relative knows what happened next: the money went fast, and in my case for various reasons, including the ridiculous prices of futons in Queens, and how you can eat only so many on-sale mealy apples and sourdough pretzels before you need a deluxe plate from a Mexican restaurant, and how you can put off calling the electric company for an account in your name only so long before your lights go off, in my case just as I began taking a shower. Not to mention that, after I bought two outfits of what even I would call pedestrian sweaters and jeans at the clothing equivalent of the 99 Cents Store ("$10 and Under," they called it), I grew tired of alternating between one decent and two nearly-identical-and-lame-looking outfits as I progressed through a week. And *laundry* costs more than you'd think when you can't borrow a roommate's detergent and the driers in your building's rainforest-damp laundromat reach room temperature at best.

It got to the point that I actually regretted not having gone back to Frank and Francine's that first night to get my stuff, since now, as far as their friend-ship went, I was well beyond the point of no return, but I wouldn't at all have minded any of those clothes I'd never worn in the Village, or another free meal of Thai and spumoni.

And: coffee. To save money, I hadn't had any since I'd begun to paint, and all I can say about this is never, ever take coffee for granted.

As far as my painting was concerned, I'd done well with volume. After three weeks, there were stacks of wrinkled-dry drawing pad pages all over my main room and bedroom, so many my path between them had shrunk to roughly ten inches wide. And there was paint on each page in those stacks, but I had no idea if any page looked decent to anyone but me, and sometimes, especially when I was tired, I myself disliked everything I'd done. I'd learned that much about painting, though: decide if it's good when you're tired.

I cannot, however, say that I'd grown tired of painting, because even though I'd curse myself about how I could work on something hours longer only to make it worse, I wouldn't feel completely awake until a brush had been in my hand for half an hour, even if I'd downed an entire liter of off-brand diet cola.

The upshot of my first three weeks living alone was that, now that they were over, rent was coming due and I needed a job. And here's where a single person's life can get tricky, because if you take your time looking for a job, you might be able to find one that pays excellent money for you to do basically noth-ing (for instance, selling Letterman tickets), but when you're faced with time pressure, you don't have the luxury of looking ad infinitum, even though your desire to live to a hundred insists you hold out for a gig that offers a 401K.

Which the grocery store where I'd bought my mealy apples didn't offer, but that's where I decided to work. Or maybe I should say where Carmen (who owned and managed the store) decided to let me work, because, as I was filling out my application and I came to the date-of-birth line, it hit me that I'd be thirty-five in four months, and I cringed not only because of the natural reluctance to tell anyone you're over thirty, but also because most of the employees there, from what I'd seen when I'd shopped, were in their early twenties, so I was worried my application would be denied on account of agism. The point is, I convinced myself I looked twenty-five—not too much of a stretch because I'd lost weight while I'd painted and weight loss makes me appear younger—and fudged the year on my birthday so I'd be twenty-five on my application, and I did land a job (Part-Time Stocker/Checker), but then, for the first couple weeks, I worried Carmen would try to verify my age with Social Security.

After a few months, though, I felt certain she never would, because she avoided Social Security so she wouldn't have to pay the tax to employ us. We were there on the sly, all of her little elves, and essentially everything there was done on the sly. When Carmen worked a register, its drawer would stay open so that whatever cash she took in would never be taxed. And our paychecks weren't checks: she'd hand us these purple envelopes, usually well past our supposed payday, and too often we'd open our envelopes and get *halves* of bills—she'd tear a hundred-dollar-bill in half and give one to me and the other to another employee, and if you tried to use one of these half-bills to buy your own groceries from her, she wouldn't accept it. And if you complained about anything, your next envelope came later than late.

"I'll pay you after closing," she'd say if you were scheduled to work a shift until seven, and we closed at eight, so it was either walk home and sit for a minute and head right back, or sit in the stockroom, in which case she'd tell you to mop. If you'd say your shift was over, she'd say, "I own this store, so when you're here, you're either working or trespassing." And she knew that we all knew she was sleeping with Johnny the Cop, and that Johnny believed whatever she said, so you'd work that extra hour in order to stay to get your purple envelope, and then, minutes before we'd close, she'd leave for an hour, then return and say, "I just deposited today's cash; I can't pay you."

Or she'd pay you all but ten dollars, and you'd mentioned the discrepancy to her, and she'd say, "All transactions are final. Take it or leave it."

And if you dared to ask for pay for the hour you'd worked while you'd waited for your envelope, she'd say, "Let's look at the schedule." She always wore turtlenecks, to hide hickeys I was quite sure, and she tugged her collar toward her ears whenever she was ready to bullshit you. "Says here," she'd say, "you weren't *scheduled* to work that hour. You can't go scheduling extra hours to support your drug habit. Should we call Johnny and discuss this with him?"

And I wasn't doing drugs, not even cough medicine, much as it was true that a joint could've helped me deal with the sight of her over-lifted face.

Plus before she'd hand you your envelope, she'd make you sign the schedule twice, once to confirm that your hours were correct, again as a receipt for your pay, and sometimes, after you'd sign twice, she'd cross out a day of your work, have you initial the cross-out, then dock your pay for that shift's worth of hours. "No initials, no envelope," she'd say, and she'd grin.

Once, about six months into working there, I got so upset I came right out and told her I hoped all of her fraud would catch up with her—and that if she fired me for saying so, I'd sue her and report her to the *Times*—and she held the schedule in front of my face and took her Wayne Newton lighter off her carton of Benson & Hedges and lit the schedule and grinned. She had this thing about Wayne Newton. Glossies of him covered her side of the customer service counter; "Daddy Don't You Walk So Fast" played twice an hour on her home-made Musak cassette. Anyway the schedule was burning, which, to me, meant I wouldn't get paid, so I reached for it, and she tossed it at my face—and my hair caught fire. I put it out with my hands before it did horrific damage, but she ran off yelling *"Michelle's burning the schedule!"*—and I had to face Johnny the Cop.

But that might be getting ahead of things. Though that was one of my problems with her: there were so many angles to her injustices, you'd get sidetracked explaining a given one. And it's hard to focus, especially on painting, when your mind is boggled by fear. Once, outside my building, I ran into that woman Sandy from across the hall, and I mentioned some of the hijinks Carmen pulled, and you'd think she, Sandy, would have listened owing to her experience as a therapist, but all she said was, "Sounds like this Carmen has issues." Then she changed the subject to how she herself was now selling insurance (rather than making sure people didn't get taken by insurance companies) in a smooth but abrupt manner that convinced me she thought I had issues because I was in my thirties yet worked at a grocery store. I couldn't blame her for this since she didn't know I also painted, and it *had* been my choice to keep my painting secret from her, but I'd kept it secret because I hadn't painted long enough to risk that, if I told her I painted, she'd insist I show her what I'd done until I'd let her see my best paintings, and then I'd have to pretend to believe her when, despite herself, she'd say, "It's good."

Not to mention I didn't want to invite her over because, with every passing day, my apartment was that much more of a hell-hole, Salsa music sandwiching me every Friday and Saturday night after the clubs in Queens closed, bath water from the hash dealer upstairs dripping onto my scalp when I bathed, mushrooms on the ceiling above my refrigerator because, apparently, the hash dealer's wife had hooked a portable wash machine to their leaking kitchen sink. I complained to the super about this more times than I cared to count, mentioning how Channel 2 had reported that mushrooms on a ceiling in Brooklyn killed some eight-year-old kid who'd done nothing but *walk under* them—and then an assistant super, three weeks after I'd quit complaining, buzzed up, walked in, pointed at the mushrooms and a DAMAGE TO PREMISES FORM, and said, "I see no mushrooms. Sign if you want me to scrub and you pay."

So I never invited Sandy over, not then or ever, and at some point, maybe two months after we'd met on the day I'd moved in, we stopped being friends, somewhat like how my first roommate in college and I had stopped but more severely: Sandy and I didn't just quit being ourselves around each other, we went cold turkey, not even saying a word. Looking back, it seems impossible that I could have met someone who was so honest about who she was and what she thought of me, and then, only two months later, without an argument, stop even saying hello to each other, but it happened.

What's even more unbelievable is that, after Sandy and I reached this impasse, I'd feel comfortable when we'd both appear on our landing and not even
glance at each other. There was something about how we'd keep our backs to
each other as we'd lock or unlock our doors that assured me she wasn't angry at
me, that instead both of our minds had clicked into an implied agreement that
we'd said everything important we could ever say to each other and there was
no point forcing conversation further. This detente felt fairly hip, especially since
we'd prefaced it by a stretch of days in which, somehow, we managed to arrange
our arrival and departure schedules so we'd never cross paths. I'll admit, however, that, during that stretch of days, I wondered if she'd died or felt ashamed
now that she was selling insurance, and that I left my door ajar for an entire
evening in order to hear if she opened hers. After I'd heard nothing and closed
my door for good that night, I felt emotionally gridlocked by embarrassment and
pride regarding my painting, my apartment, and my god-awful job.

My best attempt to explain this gridlock: When all you do is paint by yourself and work for a tyrant like Carmen, you reach the point at which you need to
love yourself like a mother loves a firstborn child, and when you realize you're
thirty-four years old and earning minimum wage, you decide that, to be fair to
the future children of the world, you probably shouldn't conceive any of them.
But then you realize that most men you'd meet wouldn't date you seriously (because men, sooner or later, tend to want to have *sons* who'll emulate them), so
you stop going to clubs, which makes you more of a hermit, though solitude, you
realize with no small amount of pride, will help you focus to paint better.

In any event, I didn't really need Sandy's friendship; I had a friend of sorts
at work, Guillermo, a forty-some-year-old guy who hadn't graduated from high
school because he wasn't quite all there. Carmen had hired him *because* he was
no PhD (she preferred her employees to be borderline G.E.D.'s so they wouldn't
question her attempts to indenture them), and on the first day I worked there,
weeks before I realized how downright evil Carmen was, he and I, during my
first ten-minute break, hid in the stockroom behind cartons of eggs and inhaled

D'Anjou pears, vanilla wafers, and half a gallon of whole milk. I'd thought to do this only because I was starved and the pears were bruised and the cookies had been torn open in shipment and the "sell by" date on the milk had already passed, and I think Guillermo joined me against his better judgment: as we sat there and ate, his ankles were actually trembling, because, as he managed to explain, he was worried we'd get caught by Carmen and fired. I think he had some kind of Bad-Boy-Coming-To-Terms-With-Mommy thing going with her, since he was fine at basic logic and pronunciation except when she'd bitch him out about one of her nonsensical rules, at which point instead of "Yes," he'd say "Yesh."

He'd never mispronounce that word otherwise, and you had to like him when he did, if for no other reason than it made you want to befriend him to try to figure him out. He had yellow-raisin-colored eyes, which, along with his name and Asian features, suggested he might have been a melting pot baby, and he often made a big, musical production out of breathing through his hair-infested nose. Sometimes the sound of his nasal breaths coaxed me to like him even more than I normally did, maybe because I felt sorry for its childishness, far more sorry than I'd feel when Carmen belittled him into a "Yesh." Or maybe I didn't feel sorry for his childishness as much as I needed to focus on childishness in general, since working with him under The Tyranny of Carmen would soon force me to face what Sandy might have called the child left in me.

Chapter 18

Maybe seven months after I'd begun working for Carmen in Astoria, Mercury dimes began showing up in the registers. I had an idea why: this Polish woman was using them to buy groceries. At least she had once. I'd been working the register that morning, and she, this Polish woman, plopped down three heads of purple cabbage, then paid with a green $10 roll of dimes. Carmen's reign of terror had me feeling paranoid (in my time there, she'd fired everyone who'd been employed there on my first day except Guillermo and me), so I feared this old woman had stuffed the roll with four inches of something fake, which would've made my drawer ten dollars short at the end of my shift (those ten dollars, of course, would have come out of my pay), so I struck the roll against the register drawer, and it split, and I heard several odd-sounding clinks. Slugs, I thought, but then I saw, on one of them, the woman on the Mercury dime, who, just as when she'd appeared on my palm when I'd been a kid, seemed to be lying asleep. She'd scared me when I'd been a kid, not because of the wings on the side of her head, but because her profile reminded me of the last snapshot in the family photo album beneath sweaters in my father's lowest dresser drawer, a polaroid of my mother lying in her casket. In fact, when I was a kid and she—the woman on the Mercury dime—had appeared on my palm, the wings on the side of her head had calmed me, because I'd believed they were a sign from some angel that my mother had flown straight to heaven.

"Problem?" the Polish woman asked, and I counted her change, gave it to her, bagged her cabbage, and played it off. I mean, as much as I wanted to, I couldn't freeze the customer line to reminisce about those dimes; Carmen, I noticed, was watching me with her arms crossed, which meant if the line grew, she'd be on me.

In a way, I was glad Carmen was watching, because the pressure from her eyes took my mind off my mother's death. Three customers later, though, when Carmen was at customer service counting cash, I realized Mercury dimes could be worth ten dollars apiece easily: I had a cousin who'd collected coins and told me classified ads had offered ten dollars and change for Mercuries long before I'd left Kankakee. So, between customers, I went for it. A ten dollar bill slipped smoothly from my purse (kept at any counter I worked since the day someone took cash from it) into the register, and then every dime from the drawer sat on my palm, and then, like a numbskull, I paused to nod at the winged woman on top of them all, hoping for the existence of my mother's soul in my friend the karmic vapor, and thinking about how, all these years later, the winged woman who was still on those dimes might empower me. After all, ten dollars times 100 is what Frank of Astoria would have called a grand.

I call myself a numbskull because, as I slid the dimes into a front pocket of my jeans, Carmen was in my face. "What are you doing?" she asked, and I shook my head, but my eyes gave me away. "Empty your pockets," she said, "or you're fired."

I should have walked immediately. In fairness to me, at the time I didn't know how much Carmen had been out to get rid of me. But still, I should've walked; a thousand dollars tax-free would have been worth it. Why I shrugged and emptied my pocket still gets me. I guess, for those few moments, while Carmen stared me down into obedience, I, sort of like Guillermo, became a Bad-Girl-Coming-To-Terms-With-Mommy. And Carmen took every coin I had in my pockets. And for grins the next Friday, a hundred from my pay.

Halfway through the end of my shift on that Friday, as I took a break in a corner of the stockroom but kept a box-cutter nearby so I could look busy if Carmen appeared, the silver doors that led to the aisles opened, and I couldn't see who it was thanks to a pallet of twenty-pound sacks of rice between whoever it was and me, and then I heard Carmen say, "Then pour the blood in this baggie, Guillermo," and I readied my box-cutter against a carton of wheat puffs. "And zip-lock it like so," she told him. "And remind her to put it under her wig. And remind her that when she falls, she should make sure her head hits the floor."

"Why would she do that?" Guillermo asked.

What's she talking about? I thought.

Carmen sighed. "So it'll burst and flow, Guillermo. Through the wig and onto the floor."

Guillermo's confusion, I was sure, was wrinkling his nose. "But I thought you wanted the floor *clean*," he said.

"That's *after* the blood spills," Carmen told him.

"Then why have her fall in the first place?" he asked.

"Guillermo, who's the boss here?"

Guillermo cleared his throat. "You."

"And I pay you, and I'm busy, so don't ruin efficiency here by asking questions. Since you asked, though, I'll tell you. Though I'm telling you as a courtesy, so you must promise to keep your trap shut about it."

No response.

"You promise?"

"Yesh."

When she leaves, I told myself, don't even ask him about this—he'll never break a promise to Mommy.

"And you understand," she said, "that if you break that promise, I'll have grounds to fire you." She said this without raising her voice, probably thinking that if she did, I'd hear her from out in the aisles, where, last she'd seen me, she'd told me to hang signs for discounts the cash register scanners would never read. "And that if I fire you," she told Guillermo now, "federal law requires me to report that you don't have a green card."

"I'm sorry, Miss Carmen. I don't need to know—"

"You asked, so I'll tell you. Which means, of course, that you'll owe me one."

"I don't want to know—"

"Our insurance company, Guillermo," she said, "requires us to practice responses to accidents. This keeps premiums from rising—see, I pay *premiums* to run this store—which allows me to let you work here without cutting your pay."

Bullshit, I thought.

"Okay," Guillermo said.

"Business is *complicated*, Guillermo. So if something around here doesn't make sense to you, trust me or find a new job."

"Okay."

"So you trust me."

"Okay."

"I'd like a yes or no answer."

"Yesh."

But why blood through a wig? I wanted to ask, though I didn't dare, because I, like Guillermo, was baked. My plan since the day I'd surrendered the Mercury dimes had been to play dumb about her rip-off scams, save at least a thousand dollars, and quit. I'd need at least a thousand to get by while I applied for another job, which I knew wouldn't come easy—asking for a recommendation from Carmen would have been employment suicide.

Unfortunately, most of the cash I'd saved from Carmen's late paydays had been eaten by investment in paint supplies. In fact, one Saturday night, with no boyfriend, no TV, no phone, and no stereo, I'd glared at the proliferating mushrooms on my ceiling and told myself that a painting of them might get me discovered, and that they therefore deserved more than watercolors on crinkled-dry sheets of art pad paper, and I took the N through Soho to Pearl Paints and waited on line behind a dozen art school students clutching their rainbows of oil paints and Visa cards, then bought my own oils in primary colors and ten "professional" canvasses (pre-stretched over frames), and six brushes with handles made out of actual wood.

My point is that, because I'd believed in my painting, my savings were basically gone, and that I knew getting fired would only strap me more tightly into my personal version of hell in Queens, so I told myself to wait until Carmen and Guillermo had left the stockroom before I sneaked out between the aisles, where I belonged. And as if Carmen heard me telling myself this, she hissed a final exhale of a Benson & Hedges, and the silver doors opened and closed.

But Guillermo was still there. I could hear his nasal breathing, which still tickled me, so, while I was stuck behind that pallet of rice, I figured why not settle back and enjoy the sound of him. I sat and listened surrounded by a goldmine of food, including, inches from me, millions of grains of goodness from the East: sure, that rice was probably stolen off a ship, but the heart of it—at least the very middle of one grain in one sack—had to be pure. And Guillermo was pure, at least void of thoughts complex enough to suspect Carmen's latest scheme, and if you listened to him work, you heard beauty: an innocent, middle-aged man breathing while working for cash to buy food to fuel that same breathing.

The goodness of that sound tempted me to watch him, so I peeked. He was crouched on the fork-lift-chipped floor, pouring beef blood (Carmen must have told the butcher to leave early the night before) from a bucket into an open zipper-top plastic bag. Or trying to. Rarely were his motor skills up to par anyway, and he was rushing, and half of the blood ran over the outside of the bag and onto his corrective shoes. He was, if you asked me, over-focused, the tip of his tongue past the left corner of his mouth, trying to English the flow of the blood into the bag. When the bucket was empty, he sealed the bag with more than enough pinches, his lips pursed, his nasal breathing louder. Then he wiped the outside of the bag with his palms, licked each of them clean, nodded, and said, "Done." I thought he was talking to me—he'd seen or heard me?—but he gave himself a thumbs-up, walked the bag to the opposite corner of the stockroom, and placed it so carefully behind the cartons of olives he couldn't have sensed me sneak out through the silver doors.

Under the florescent lights that made the expired frozen shrimp look pink, I checked the shoplifting-prevention mirror (Carmen was too cheap to run the mounted video cam) and saw her facing the register between aisles 2 and 3. Barely confident she hadn't seen me return, which would have given her grounds to fire me (which, even though I despised working there, would have put me in the worst quandary), I began doing what she'd ordered, taping up her deceptive SALE! signs.

For the record, one of her scams with those signs was that they proclaimed sale prices when, in reality, her scanners at the registers would ring up pre-sale prices. If a customer caught onto this, whoever worked the register had standing orders to say Carmen had forgotten to change the price in the scanner's computer, then punish the customer by taking ample time to lock the register, leave the counter to check the price on the shelf, get the key to void the overcharge, use the key to do so, document the void on a void form, and re-ring the item on sale. This punishment usually worked toward Carmen's advantage: people on line behind the customer who'd complained would grumble so much about having to wait, the customer rarely again mentioned an overcharge.

Anyway I had two SALE! signs taped when the shoplifting-prevention mirror showed a woman standing beside Carmen, Carmen herself pointing to a register's buttons as if explaining them. Training my replacement, I thought, but then I convinced myself I was wrong: maybe my threat to report her to the *Times* had her more worried than I'd thought.

Then came the minute during which I considered the roots of her viciousness. Bad childhood? I wondered, but mine had been bad. In fact, my father was like Carmen. To him, nothing about me was ever right. Maybe he'd treated me like that, I thought as I taped up a sign, because my mother had died giving me birth, a detail that, for most of my life, I'd tried to keep out of my mind. On the other hand, when I was twelve, my father and I had had a heart-to-heart about her death. *"It wasn't your fault, Michelle,"* he'd said. *"You were an infant, for God's sake."* Though days after that talk, he returned to treating me as if he wished I were gone. You'll never please him, I'd decided in The Reliant on the way to Manhattan.

And now I'm taking flak from Carmen, I thought as I stuck a sign beneath a can of bean soup. People like me leave one tyrant only to seek out another. Carmen's meanness, I decided, was why I'd *chosen* to follow her orders.

I continued taping, though. Guilt about what I did for her paled beside my fear of her. And while I taped, I had a fantasy about the Mercury dimes I'd given to her. Actually it wasn't as much a fantasy as it was a replay of what had occurred except with a happy ending of me keeping the dimes and telling her off. Then, after imagining how many oils I could buy with the money I would have gotten for the dimes, I flat-out undermined one of her scams.

See, another Carmen trick with the SALE! signs was that I put, say, a SALE! HALF OFF KRAZGUARD KETCHUP! sign under the shelf of *Kravetts* ketchup, which cost more than Krazguard when Krazguard wasn't on sale. She'd have me do this so rushed or semi-literate customers (altogether most of them) would buy the Kravetts instead of the Krazguard five feet away. Of course, any customer sharp enough to match a SALE! sign with its actually corresponding product still had to fight the scanner that beeped up the wrong price, but anyway I protested Carmen's tyranny by taping the signs *directly beneath the items to which they referred.* After all, I thought, if I am wired to seek tyrants, shouldn't I force myself to fight injustice?

Soon I was near the registers, out of Carmen's sight but within earshot of what she was saying. "And you take the customer's money," she told the woman beside her. "And push this button, and the drawer opens. Always take the money first, Olga, because if your drawer doesn't square with the total on the tape at the end of your shift, the difference comes out of your check."

She *is* my replacement, I thought. Olga. No green card. $4.65 an hour.

"And if you see any old coins, give them to me."

"Old coins?" Olga asked, pronouncing it *Olt coinz*, reminding me of better days—living with Etta.

"Yes," Carmen said. "They're lighter and worn smooth."

"And I give them to you?"

"Yes. Because they're worthless. They're out of circulation, so they're essentially counterfeit. I don't want to cheat our customers. Or you, if you ever make change for yourself. So as a courtesy, I replace them with cash from my pocket."

The irony of that lie—Carmen emptying *her* pocket after she'd forced me to empty mine of those Mercury dimes—propelled me to the customer side of that counter. "Olga?" I said. "I'm Michelle. I work the registers, too, so if you have any questions when Carmen is busy, say—burning our schedules?—feel free to ask me."

And I couldn't believe I'd said it, but now that I had, I steadied myself to see what would happen next, and Carmen grabbed the intercom mike, tugged her turtleneck toward her ears, and, full volume, said, "Guillermo?"

Here we go, I thought. A woman with a bag of blood under her wig will appear, slip, and fall. And Carmen will blame me—in order to fire me. And the woman who'll fall is Olga.

But Olga wasn't moving. She was smiling at me. Her smile appeared real, nothing like the flat smirk on Carmen's face. Olga seemed poised to befriend me, and I could have used another friend. But if I didn't ignore her to watch my ass, I was history. And if Johnny the Cop believed it was my fault that a woman slipped and fell, maybe he'd hold me in jail, at least for a night, on some bogus negligence/manslaughter charge?

"Michelle," Carmen said, aiming her smirk at me. "I need the Baby Soft here. It's advertised on sale and customers are asking for it. I told you to bring it out two days ago, so you'd better do it now."

Of course, she'd never told me to bring out any Baby Soft.

"And make it fast," she said now.

"You want it in the t.p. aisle, right?" I asked as nicely as I could.

"No." She pinched her turtleneck, a shamrock green one that day. "I want both cartons of it in front of this counter. In plain view for the customers, who, of course, always come first."

"But they'll look for it where it belongs," I said.

"Michelle, who owns this store?"

Okay, I thought. Bring out the Baby Soft. Do it quickly but carefully.

I began down aisle two. Three customers stood in it, all men, two bald or balding—no woman wearing a wig. And, as rushed as I was, I excused myself past each without touching them.

Then I was in the stockroom. Guillermo was nowhere. I remembered my first day at work, when he and I had shared pears, cookies, and milk. I ran to the corner to check for the zipper-top plastic bag, but it was gone. I checked another corner behind canned salmon where he kept his lunch, but nothing was there either. It's with Guillermo, I thought. Out in the aisles. He's giving it to the woman who will fake the fall. Then I realized that as I'd excused myself past the three men, I'd forgotten to check the shoplifting-prevention mirror for Guillermo or a woman wearing a wig.

"*Both cartons, Michelle,*" Carmen shouted over the intercom. "*Hurry.*"

Side by side, the two Baby Soft cartons were too wide to fit through an aisle. Stacked one on top of the other, they'd never allow me to see over them. That, I realized, was Carmen's plan: rushing toward her with stacked cartons blocking my view, I wouldn't see a woman with a baggie of blood under her wig, and she'd fake a fall and a cracked skull, and I'd be fired. Johnny the Cop would be at the scene, and if I challenged Carmen, he'd arrest me for assault, battery, or disturbing the peace. If it came to that, Guillermo would witness. Under oath, he'd sing harmony with Carmen's lies, and then I'd be considered fired with cause, and I'd never collect a penny of unemployment. Goodbye, Astoria, I thought. Goodbye, Manhattan. I never even saw Staten Island. I imagined myself on the bus back to Kankakee, then running into Thom and knowing the thought behind his smile: *You failed in New York because you think too much.*

"Michelle," Carmen's voice said. "*We need both boxes now.*"

Okay, I thought. Just don't carry them. Stack them and slide them slowly and crane your neck around them to watch for a woman wearing a wig.

I heaved one carton onto the other, then checked through the scratched plastic windows in the silver doors. No one was out there. Unless the woman wearing a wig was crouched directly beneath the windows, I was fine. I knelt and spied through the crack under the doors, saw nothing but fluorescent-lit tile, heard nothing but Wayne Newton whine.

Then I stood behind the cartons. Baby Soft, I thought. Why, at this moment, must I be reminded of babies and mothers?

Forget your mother, I told myself. Push these cartons past her death and forget her for good. Push carefully and leave the cartons beside Carmen, then tell her you quit and walk out of this godforsaken store.

I pushed an inch, then two. The doors parted. "*Let's go, Michelle,*" the intercom said. Then I was out under the lights, still pushing. You can prevent this, I thought. Just don't touch anyone. The boxes were cooperating but not perfectly stacked. I evened them out, then saw a customer walk toward me, a woman I'd never seen before, whose silver hair shone like gift ribbon: maybe a wig. I hugged the top carton and smiled and said "Careful," and she returned a wiry smile and continued toward me, and I fought the cartons to prop her shoulder as she fell, but her bulk was too much for both of us: she was down. She hadn't even touched the boxes. *Then* she screamed—and knocked the left side of her head against the floor. Through the wig, blood ran. "I'm sorry" was what came out of my mouth. The blood was puddling. Had anyone heard me? I wondered. The puddle expanded, beef-blood to me, but red enough to appear human to a stranger.

"*Attention,*" Carmen's voice called. "*We have an emergency. Please remain calm. Do not attempt to assist the victim.*"

The two bald men appeared at the far end of the aisle. They aren't customers, I thought. They're witnesses for Carmen. They ran toward me as I knelt and reached for the wig—but they had me. "Stay calm," one said. "Your manager said not to assist her." I tried to wrestle free, but they pinned me, and Carmen appeared, followed by Johnny the Cop and Guillermo. Johnny hadn't bothered to sound his siren. Olga, at the far end of the aisle, studied the woman with the wig, who kept her eyes shut as Johnny and Carmen propped her against the canned yams.

Carmen faced me and said, "Michelle, I told you to be careful."

Olga, arms crossed, gaped at me: to her, I was as guilty as Mercury dimes were worthless.

You're fired, I thought. It's over. Forget Carmen's hell and face your own.

Chapter 19

Six blocks from having seen Carmen for the last time, I felt light. Sure, I was job-less and therefore earmarked for Kankakee, but Kankakee, I told myself, might be tolerable now that I was learning to face my mother's death. If anything her death had been my father's fault in a way—for getting her pregnant in the first place. Like me, she'd had a small frame, which might have had something to do with me getting stuck as she'd struggled to give me birth. *He* should have thought twice nine months earlier; I'd had no choice but to be born.

And no law, I reminded myself, requires wives to bear children. In fact, from everything I'd heard from friends of mine who were parents, their children more or less killed them anyway. Friends of mine with kids tended to end con-versations about parenthood by saying, "Don't get me wrong, my children are the most wonderful thing that's ever happened to me," but they usually tagged this on after they'd whined profusely about what they'd endured as parents: fi-nancial pressure, the need to stay home, the resultant hatred—*hatred*—of their spouses, as well as infrequent and rote intercourse, and the inevitable suspicion of affairs.

And yes, I knew I wouldn't exist had my parents decided not to have children, but I also knew that, had they decided not to, my mother wouldn't have died. These two realities had never been easy for me to consider simultaneously, but as I walked on toward my apartment, I no longer ignored my mother's death due to guilt. Instead I conceived of her intellectually, as if she were someone who'd made history. I didn't kill her, I thought. I didn't kill her. Death waited for everyone, including me.

If anything, my life was the problem to face. Now that I was emancipated from Carmen, I did not want to live out my days in Astoria, since Astoria, it was now clear, was just a place where suckers survived day to day while they kidded themselves about living in New York. The real New York, it was now irrefutably clear, was Manhattan, and anyplace else, even if one of the boroughs, might as well have been Kankakee.

That's why, roughly a block from my building, when I saw Ernest Coolridge, I felt somewhat thrown. Here I'd been, thinking about people frustrated by eternal residence *just outside* of Manhattan, and there he was, walking toward me as if he were *in* Manhattan: chin held high, daring whoever saw him to wonder why, beneath his ascot, a chunk of his jaw was missing. My impulse as soon as I recognized him was to dash ahead and hug him, but he was looking across the street so intently I sensed he was trying to avoid me. I walked faster still toward him, and when we were ten feet apart, I said "Hey, Ernest," and he looked me in the eye, nodded, and passed me. I stopped and turned and yelled "Ernest? It's me! Michelle!"

He kept on, and I ran toward him. When I reached him, he had stopped to lift a coin from beneath the tip of his loafer. Pinching the coin as he recognized me, he addressed me with the grin of a kid in Harlem who's found a hundred dollar bill, his throat grinding up noises it had made in Manhattan when he'd been excited or cross. He grabbed my wrist, pressed the coin onto my palm, pointed to it—a Mercury dime, to my disbelief—then pointed to me, his way, I guessed, of saying, "THIS IS YOURS."

"Thanks, Ernest," I said, and I thought to kiss him but instead struggled for words to tell him what a Mercury dime meant to me just then, and he pulled out his notepad and wrote:

WHY ARE YOU
IN ASTORIA?

"I live here," I said. "In this building, in fact. And you?"

He squeezed the notepad as he wrote, then had a thought out:

VISITING A LADY

"Oh?" I said, and he winked, then scribbled:

A LOOKER

"Ah," I said, but I realized that, if he was still engaged to Joyce, this development might not be as good as I'd made it sound. "For business or pleasure?" I asked.

He scribbled for so long I was sure he was explaining that he'd broken up with Joyce, who, I realized, might have been the only person willing to take care of him if his cancer returned. Altogether he filled three pages with words, a good number of them deleted with angrily etched lines, then turned back to the first of the three pages, stood beside me, held the pad the ideal distance from my face, and used a manicured finger to guide my eyes, flipping to the next page after I'd nod:

I WAS GOING

TO ASK HER TO
SUBLEASE
MY APARTMENT.

SO WE COULD BE
"FRIENDS" THERE

AFTER I
MARRY JOYCE.
IT'S COMPLICATED
BUT JOYCE AND I
HAVE
AN UNDERSTANDING.

(JOYCE HAS
BOYFRIENDS TOO). (?)

I'M SO GLAD TO
SEE YOU.

WHAT DO YOU
THINK?

"About...what?" I asked.

His throat squealed, from impatience, I guessed, and he flipped back a page
and pointed to "AN UNDERSTANDING."

"If you have this understanding," I asked, "why get married?"

He held up a finger, then wrote:

JOYCE'S CO-OP

REQUIRES IT.

WE NEED TO LIVE

THERE TOGETHER
TO SAVE $.

(+ MY APARTMENT'S TOO

He continued on an unmarked page:

SMALL FOR US).

BUT,

AS A WOMAN,

DO YOU
THINK I SHOULD
SUBLET MY PLACE TO A

Again, he flipped ahead:

GIRLFRIEND?

When I saw that last word, I laughed, and he did, too, and as our laughter deepened, I thought I was relieving myself of my frustrations as Carmen's employee but sensed there was more at stake than that, because I laughed so hard I couldn't catch my breath. I remembered my flare-up of asthma at Frank and Francine's, and how Ernest had struggled to breathe whenever Joyce had chided him, and then I could breathe but he and I were still laughing, perhaps, it seemed, at memories we had in common, and all that came to mind was the mouth-to-mouth we'd shared while Etta's building burned.

Finally, we calmed ourselves. And he wrote:

> I GUESS
> THAT'S MY
> ANSWER.

"What do you mean?" I asked.

> NO
> SUBLEASE FOR THE
> GIRLFRIEND.

"I really don't know, Ernest," I said.

> IN FACT,
> THE GIRLFRIEND'S
>
> HISTORY.

"That would probably make things less complicated," I said. "But I really can't say—"

He pressed a finger against my lips, then crammed more than usual onto a notepad page:

> I
> WAS

NERVOUS
WALKING
DOWN THIS
BLOCK ANYWAY.
BECAUSE MY GUT KNEW I
WAS ON MY WAY TO ASKING
FOR TROUBLE.

"Are you sure?" I asked.

He nodded and broke into a private bout of strangled laughter, and I wanted to laugh too but felt sobered by how I knew he'd just broken up with a woman who was now clueless about her future without him. Then he held up a finger, composed himself, and adopted a grave expression, and wrote:

THANK YOU
FOR HELPING ME
DECIDE.

YOU'RE

AN ANGEL.

"Thank *you*," I said. "For calling me that."

He bowed sheepishly, completed a smooth about-face, and walked off toward 30th Avenue, and I found myself in one of those situations where you want to stop someone from leaving but know that, if you'd try, your connection with that person might stop feeling as close to perfect as it does. Instead, I watched his frame shrink as he neared the end of the block, where he stopped in front of traffic, waiting, I was sure, to cross 30th Avenue and continue on to 36th to hang a right toward the subway, and I envied his Manhattan address but pitied him as well: he'd needed to visit Astoria—and run into *me*—to make a decision about love.

Then the traffic in front of him cleared, and he was moving, but headed back toward me. He wants his girlfriend, I thought. He decided to break up with Joyce. I thought to duck into my building so he wouldn't need to explain himself to me, but he waved, calling, it seemed, for me to wait for him. He held his notepad in front of him, then finally grew close enough for me to see what he'd returned to say:

DO <u>YOU</u>

WANT MY
APARTMENT?

Had he asked this seven months earlier, I would have said yes with abandon, but it wasn't seven months earlier. It was now, and I was thirty-five, and my ego no longer obscured how I couldn't paint worth a damn, and, thanks to Carmen, I no longer had an income, just barely enough cash for a bus ride to Kankakee.

"I'd love to live there," I told him. "But I don't think I can. I just lost my job, Ernest, and I think it's time for me to leave. New York, I mean. I mean, I think I'm going back. You know, to..."

I hoped I'd said enough, but he wrote:

IDAHO?

"Illinois," I said. "But you get my point."
He nodded, then wrote:

WE CAN

MAKE AN

ARRANGEMENT

FOR YOU TO

New page:

LIVE

IN MY PLACE FOR <u>FREE</u>.

"Ernest," I said. "Don't take this wrong. But I don't think it would be good for either of us if I were your girlfriend."

He rolled his eyes theatrically, throwing back his head and miming the word No! Then he tried to hug me—but I stiffened despite myself, and he stepped back. With focused determination, he wrote:

YOU'RE

LIKE A

DAUGHTER!

I kept my eyes on the page until I was sure my face wouldn't reveal guilt about the quasi-sexual thoughts I'd had about him. Also, now that I'd made so much progress past my guilt about my mother's death, I felt *beyond* my status as a daughter, and it irked me that Ernest might have thought I needed a surrogate parent. Still, I enjoyed remnants of how perfectly I'd felt after he'd called me an angel and walked off, so I said, "That means a lot to me, Ernest. If I'd live in your place, how would the arrangement work?"

He pointed to the stoop of a house across the street, where we sat as he wrote to explain that he needed to keep his apartment because, as much as he loved

Joyce and wanted to marry her, his experience as an ex-Yankee told him never to put all his "EMOTIONAL EGGS IN ANYONE ELSE'S BASKET." He'd had affairs with too many married women, he explained, whose motivation to "BE WITH" him had been based (as he now saw it) on little more than childish impulses to seduce someone famous. On top of this, his apartment was tiny, even for a studio in Manhattan, and its only bathroom was a "SHARED" one down the hall, but rent there was "CHEAP," so if he'd give up the apartment, he'd never be able to get it back, which would mean, as far as his relationship to Joyce went, he'd lose "LEVERAGE." After I read that word, I wanted to chastise him on Joyce's behalf, but then I remembered how she'd henpecked him when he'd tried to fix my shade at Etta's place, and I empathized with his strategy and more or less took his side. The arrangement that would allow me to live there for free was one he himself had made on and off over the years whenever he'd needed "MONEY TO BURN": he knew businessmen who'd pay "GOOD CASH" for a place where they could "NAP" during lunch hours or just after work, so all I'd need to do was leave the apartment for "AN HOUR A FEW TIMES A MONTH"; otherwise, I could live there—rent-free—as if the place were mine.

This conversation, even before it ended, did not sit well with me for several obvious reasons: *affairs* went on in that apartment, so if I lived there, I'd be helping men cheat, plus there was the issue of hygiene. I asked him about hygiene as if it were a minor detail, and he answered immediately:

> THEY
> DO IT
> ON
> A COMFORTER.
>
> (& CLEAN
> UP WHEN THEY'RE
> DONE.)

That last line made it difficult to mention my concern about helping men cheat. It was simply up to me to ignore marital infidelity if I wanted to remain in New York—*and in the only borough that counted*. And I was sure Ernest knew that if I didn't take his offer, the next person he'd run into would. I was facing, I realized, a moral decision, the kind you can make quickly in favor of what you want to do only if you believe in Existentialism. And I tried that for a moment or two, but the result was a sense that I was dodging something I should face. Then I remembered how I'd hoped my mother's soul had been infused into my friend the karmic vapor, and how Carmen had taken my Mercury dimes and how Ernest, as soon as he'd run into me, had given me the Mercury dime I could no longer feel in my fist. That was more than coincidence, I thought. Had my mother, through the karmic vapor, *sent* Ernest to Astoria to make me the offer? Had that been why he'd used the word daughter? Did *she* want me to live in Manhattan—even if jerks as heartless as my father had affairs behind my closed door?

"Ernest?" I said. "I'm interested."

Chapter 20

As with most offers I'd encountered since I'd left Kankakee, there were details that did not come to mind initially but needed to be settled in advance. I knew, from experience when I'd ignored these kinds of details, that the best way to prevent them from inflating into nightmares was to ask as many questions as possible, so as Ernest and I rode the N into Manhattan, I asked away: How would I know when these men wanted to stop by? If I weren't there, how would they get in? Would I have to talk to these men? How would I know when they'd left?

From Ernest's point of view, that last question was easy: he kept a Statue of Liberty refrigerator magnet on the outside of the apartment's doorframe, and as I'd leave after I'd let a "GUEST" in, I would make sure the magnet was vertical—and then, when the guest would leave, he'd turn it so it was horizontal. As far as my need to speak with anyone, Ernest explained, the people who used the apartment preferred privacy, so protocol suggested an exchange of nods at most. As for how I'd know when someone wanted to stop by and how people would have access if I weren't there, Ernest admitted this indeed was a rub: I *wouldn't know* if someone wanted to come over in advance, because everyone involved agreed it was best not to rely on scheduling through written notes or calls; in fact, I needed to be home between one and two in the afternoon, and then again between five and six in the evening, but only on Mondays, Wednesdays, and Thursdays.

If that were the extent of my commitment, I figured, the arrangement could have been worse, since the hours at issue were far short of nine-to-five, and I'd be required to *do* even less than I had when I'd sold Letterman tickets, a job that, thanks to my slavery at the hands of Carmen, returned to memory as the best of my life. So I asked more questions, about run-of-the-mill amenities such as heat ("STEAM") and air-conditioning ("PORTABLE BUT FREEZING") and laundry ("RIGHT DOWN THE BLOCK, VERY HOT DRIERS"). By now we were off the train and on the shaded sidewalk on 56th, and then we hung a left onto Eighth Avenue and he pointed west, at a six-story building that had stood, it seemed, for at least a century, which, to me at the moment, meant it would remain there forever. I thought about why Ernest wanted his apartment kept in his name, and I realized that, if he and Joyce didn't stick out their marriage, he'd want back in and I'd be out, and all at once I became their marriage's biggest fan. Then we were at the security door, and he fished keys from a front pocket and let us onto the ground floor, a narrow hallway with aluminum mailboxes on the wall to the right. He checked his mail—an electric bill—and I thought, This is real. His keys, as he pocketed them, reminded me that he'd worked as Etta's super only some seven blocks down, and I remembered bathing her as well as how ticklish I'd felt when Tino had licked the skin beneath my nostrils, then asked, "How's Etta, anyway?"

Ernest stopped short of the elevator, pulled in a long breath, and wrote three letters on his pad:

R.I.P.

"You're kidding," I said.

He kept our eyes locked so long I was sure he'd burst into a grin. But he stepped back and studied me like a father absorbing a daughter's reaction to the very worst possible news.

"Oh, no," I said.

He nodded twice and released a sigh, and the elevator doors opened, and he let me on first and pushed four. As we rose, it struck me that the elevator wasn't much larger than a coffin itself, and my mother came to mind but I reminded myself I was no longer anyone's child, and we reached the fourth floor, where the doors remained shut. Ernest grabbed a steel handle on what I'd thought was the uptown wall of the elevator but was actually another door, which he pushed open. We faced a corridor twice the width of the hallway on the ground floor, this one done in black and white checkerboard tiles. Directly in front of us stood a card table covered with stacks of stapled packets of paper disheveled by a breeze that ran between the propped open windows at either end of the corridor; taped to the edge of the table was a laser-printed sign that said SIDES. Ernest led me down the right-hand half of the corridor, and we reached an enameled black door, and he again found his keys and unlocked three deadbolts and opened the door and groped for a light switch, and we both faced filth from 1959. A balding velvet couch sat against a wall at most five feet away from us—Ernest stepped immediately to his right to free me to follow him in and close the door behind us—and the room, windowless, was lit only by one of those low-hanging, single-bulb fixtures common in hideout warehouses in gangster films. The apartment, however, was no warehouse. Just to the right of the couch was a salad bowl of a sink, two dorm-size refrigerators stacked one on top of the other, and a portable wardrobe rack loaded with sports jackets, shirts, and pants. To the left was a hotplate on a cable box on a TV on a hi-fi so old I doubted it worked. The walls had been yellowed by nicotine. Beneath our feet was the only open floor space— what a positive thinker might call the living room—but all I could think as I gazed at the walls was: Living here is how he got cancer.

But you are, I reminded myself, in Manhattan. Ernest pulled a green comforter off a wooden hanger on the wardrobe rack, spread it over the couch, found a notepad on the sink, and wrote:

> THE MEN
> WILL COVER
> THE COUCH
> LIKE SO
> BEFORE THEY
> DO ANYTHING.

Which confirmed that the couch was the bed—for me and repeated acts of untold seediness.

"And they hang it up there before they leave?"

> ALWAYS.

"And they don't leave a mess."

> NEVER.
> PLUS I KEEP MY OWN
> PILLOW & BLANKETS
> IN A SUITCASE

He nodded at the wardrobe rack.

> BEHIND THERE.
> YOU'D PUT
> YOURS THERE—
> THEY WON'T

<u>TOUCH</u>
THEM.

"Well that's...reasonable," I said. To buy time in which to adopt the open-mindedness I'd need to live there, I asked, "What are 'sides'?"

He jotted on a new page, tore it off, and held it between two fingers in front of my face:

LINES FOR
ACTORS.

(THERE ARE
REHEARSAL STUDIOS
DOWN THE HALL.)

"Real actors?" I asked. "I mean, like Meryl Streep?"

He shrugged, and I stepped toward the couch and scrutinized it for stains. I saw an arguable crumb at most, though half a dozen dust-bunny-covered roach motels had been stacked between an arm of the couch and the sink. I leaned over to sniff the couch, telling myself that however it smelled would decide whether Manhattan still beat Kankakee.

It smelled good, like cedar.

"I kind of like it here, Ernest," I said, and he flipped to a new page and wrote:

AL PACINO
SAT
ON THAT
COUCH.

"Really?"

WE SMOKED

CIGARS.

"Recently?"

JUST BEFORE
DOG
DAY AFTERNOON.

I'm not the type to get star-struck, but I have to admit: this background information erased most of the doubt about where I wanted to live.

"When can I start?" I asked.

Ernest studied the hardwood floor. A hairpin, I noticed, was jammed between two of the floorboards. He slid his hand beneath a couch cushion, removed a set of keys linked by a knotted bread-bag tie, and pressed it onto my palm—beside my Mercury dime.

Chapter 21

There was no doubt I felt at home when I wanted to have a party. After all, I'd rarely even considered the prospect of parties until I'd lived someplace long enough to have ironed out the essentials of getting through an average day. After slightly more than a month in Ernest's apartment, though, my essentials were smooth. I'd discovered an A & P and a perfectly greasy take-out Chinese place on Ninth Avenue, a Duane Reade on 56th and Broadway, and a pizza place on Eighth Avenue that stayed open all night. There was also a Korean deli right next door that didn't open until eight in the morning, but this had an upside: their sandwich rolls were delivered in cardboard boxes to the space just inside my building's security door at four in the morning (the bakery delivery-truck driver had a key), and sometimes, when I couldn't sleep, I'd run through the dark corridor on my floor and take the elevator down and slide a roll past the four flaps of that particular day's box. Sometimes the rolls still held an oven's warmth, and after I'd return to my apartment and lock up, I'd savor that warmth and feel cared for.

A week before my desire to have the party took hold, I'd earned cash doing odd jobs for Ernest when he needed help being a super (I would, for example, hold a flashlight while he re-wired a building's pitch-black basement), so the party would, I decided, include him, as well as Joyce. Maybe it would also include Sarah and Walt for the sake of a good-sized crowd, though attendance didn't trouble me all that much since, in a pinch, I could try to meet the actors who auditioned for parts in the studios down the corridor and ask if they wanted a cast party.

This party, I imagined, would spill into the corridor and out the windows at both ends of it, then crawl up the rusted fire escapes to the roof, where a memorable time was virtually guaranteed, which I knew since that's where I now spent evenings. Up there, I'd lose the cooped-up feeling I often had during the day, because you could see past the Hudson or watch the strings of white headlights on Eighth Avenue headed uptown, as well as the delivery bikes and prostitutes and dope dealers you'd turned down during your afternoon walk. No matter how grand the city appeared from that vantage point, though, a faint but growing nervousness would overtake me, especially when I'd realize someone in a nearby building taller than mine might be looking down at me: the tons of concrete and bricks and water towers above would belittle me. I'd smoke more than usual on that roof, and often I'd bring along wine and assure myself I sipped it only to prime myself for the party, but my nervousness, I sometimes admitted, lay in the fact that I again lived in Manhattan, where I felt destined to be, and where, as a result, something crucial seemed bound to happen. Impatience, I supposed, was what I felt, but there was more to it than that, including hope in love and the shock you tap into when your age comes to mind and you feel cheated by all the years you wasted to find yourself.

Anyhow I wanted to have a party, and a wrinkle in making arrangements toward that end was that I didn't have a phone: I'd asked Ernest if it would be all right if I had one hooked up, and he'd said no. He'd explained that I couldn't have one because of the understanding he'd reached with the men who used my apartment; no one, himself included, wanted a soul to be able to trace any calls made from there. This understanding of theirs no doubt fueled my burgeoning nervousness, which probably led me to spend more time on the roof, and the more time I spent up there, the less I spent socializing. Now and then Ernest would ask me to meet him and Joyce—or sometimes only him—at any of several after-hours places, and sometimes I accepted his invitations, but most of those places catered to retired, divorced people who sported outdated clothes and wads of cash and discussed bets on the Yankees and chain-smoked enough to make me want to quit cigarettes. Something I learned by going to those clubs: Ernest had lost gobs of money by gambling on the Yankees.

The party aside, I wanted a phone simply to have contact with the outside world, Kankakee included, so without mention to Ernest, I signed up for a cell phone that felt good to own except when I'd see it beside the cable box and realize I hadn't used it for a week. Maybe my stint as a hermit in Astoria had cemented a shyness I couldn't crack. I don't know. It didn't help that the tenants in my building seemed unionized to avoid conversation on the elevator (I'd say hello and they'd rivet their eyes on the floor), and that the only actors in the corridor who greeted me were extremely short men, and that I knew the plight of the short man who's desperate to date an even shorter woman. Thom had been, as my friends used to say, a member of the five-four-and-under-club, and once during an argument, he told me the only reason he'd asked me out in the first place was because of my height. I'd always assured myself he hadn't meant this—that he'd lied in exasperation—but when a height-challenged actor would greet me in the corridor, Thom's words would come to mind and I'd grow awkwardly terse. So maybe six weeks after I first imagined a party centered in my apartment, the idea of befriending actors for the sake of attendance had lost oomph, even despite the bottle of vodka I'd bought to begin a stock of beverages.

To be completely truthful about the demise of the party, though, I'd have to add that, maybe twenty minutes after I bought that bottle, something crucial finally did happen. And I'd like to say it was good, but it wasn't, not any of it, and as much as I'll always value my thoughtfulness, I wish I could clear my mind of what I witnessed then.

What I'm trying to say is that someone might have died in my apartment. And the reason I think she might have is that, just before five on a Thursday evening in August, after I bought the vodka and returned to my building and took the elevator to my floor and hung the right down the corridor, I checked the Statue of Liberty magnet on the doorframe, and it was vertical, which meant a man and a woman were still in my apartment—past their hour there. This troubled me because it had never happened before—and because, for all I knew, *another* couple would stop by at five, which could mean a conflict that would involve me way beyond my job description.

I headed for the bathroom down the corridor figuring I'd smoke there until I heard the door to my apartment open and close, but when I reached the bathroom door I realized that, of course, the key to the bathroom was in my apartment, which irked me. To pass time until they left, I climbed out the window that faced the rear of the building and ascended the fire escape. That afternoon's heat clung to the roof, and tar stuck to my shoes, and resentment quickly overcame my patience. If I were flexible enough to look the other way about a strange man's dalliance in my apartment, I thought, the least he could do was follow Ernest's rules. I considered a sip of vodka to jumpstart the grandeur the roof offered at night, but I hate vodka when it's warm, but mostly I felt used because some jackass *lingered* with a woman he'd never introduce to his wife.

Assert yourself, I thought, and I climbed back down the fire escape, then swung my legs over the window sill at the end of the corridor—and as I ducked my head to get all the way inside, I glimpsed a woman's legs sliding over the checkerboard tiles around the corner toward the elevator. I told myself she was an actor being dragged by another actor as they rehearsed for an audition, but something green had covered her legs down to her shins, the same shade of green as the comforter I never touched on Ernest's wardrobe rack.

No, I thought, and I stepped backwards toward the window. I groped for, found, and sat on the sill behind me, then maneuvered my legs over it and ducked under the pane, most of me outside when I saw Ernest poke his head past the gap in the corridor wall that led to the elevator, glance to his right, then face me just as I began up the fire escape. He might not have seen me but probably had, and I scrambled up the flights of stairs despite their rust and wobble. Then I was dashing across the roof, under all of that August sunshine. If Ernest had seen me and what I'd seen had been real, he would, I feared, be climbing the fire escape to deal with me, and I wanted to see the fire escape to know if he were coming up, but if he were coming up, I didn't want him to find me. As fast as I was running, I was trapped. I stopped behind the squat brick hut that was the top of the elevator shaft, then hid behind the Eighth Avenue side of it hoping I wouldn't hear footsteps but wondering if softened tar made footsteps inaudible, and then I moved to the downtown side of the hut and sat with my back to it, facing what I now recognized as the whitewashed rear of what once had been Etta's building. Why did it have to burn? I thought. I opened the vodka and swigged, then spit out whatever I could. I lit a cigarette, poured more of the vodka over the roof, and positioned the bottle near my face: if Ernest appeared, I'd look up at him as if I'd been drinking there for hours, then match his lies or truths with my own.

Then I tried to conceive of what to do next, but came up blank. After all the thinking I'd done over the course of my life, I could not will my mind to address the fact that I'd seen a woman being dragged down my corridor to the elevator, and that Ernest now knew I'd seen her, and that, as a result, he—and whoever had dragged the woman—preferred I disappear. I remained still, holding the bottle inches from my lips, listening for footsteps, moving only now and then to ash. I tried to convince myself that what I'd seen in the corridor hadn't been real, and that, had it been real, it wasn't what I thought, though I sensed I was trying to convince myself of this because I'd witnessed something far more horrific than I'd imagined. Eventually, of course, I would need to leave the roof, and finally I decided that, for safety's sake, I'd use the fire escape on the Eighth Avenue side of the building—so that if Ernest appeared in my path as I descended, we'd be in view of pedestrians and traffic, which would limit what he—and whoever—could do to me.

At some point I thought, Go down now. Before it gets dark. But I couldn't. Finally I moved, but only to stand. I didn't want to step into view of anyone. I remembered what I'd often thought about buildings taller than mine—someone inside one could have been looking down at me—and I flailed my arms as I ran toward the fire escape on the Eighth Avenue side, climbed down as steadily as I could, raised the window to my corridor higher than it had been propped, and lowered myself onto the black and white tiles. As if facing the end of an average day, I checked the Statue of Liberty magnet on the doorframe, which was now horizontal: the man, the woman, and Ernest were probably gone.

I'd lost all but a scrap of my desire to go inside. But dammit, I thought, I live here. Feigning nonchalance poorly, I unlocked and opened the door and strode in. I left the door ajar because I wanted to be able to leave. The place smelled like a swimming pool. From bleach? I thought. I peeked behind Ernest's wardrobe rack—no one. The floorboards were cleaner than ever: if there had been blood, it was gone.

I closed the door and locked one deadbolt, then all of them. Maybe, I told myself, she overdosed and fell and cut herself on the hi-fi. And the man with her revived her but hadn't been able to stop the bleeding, and he and Ernest cabbed her to Roosevelt Hospital. They hadn't called an ambulance because, in Manhattan, people die waiting for help to come to them.

Anything's possible, I told myself. And this would have happened, I kept trying to believe, whether or not I had lived here.

Chapter 22

Part of me still clung to my love of Manhattan while the rest of me avoided the stillness in my apartment. I spent more time outdoors, taking walks during the day to neighborhoods I'd never seen, like Spanish Harlem and Battery Park and the surprisingly quiet streets around the United Nations. I passed evenings on top of my building, where, to forestall memories of the woman being dragged, I'd try not to look at the brick hut I'd sat behind when I'd poured vodka over the edge of the roof. Instead I'd stand beside the top of the fire escape on the rear of the building, facing west, romanticizing my past in Kankakee, waiting, after the sun went down, for whichever stars might show. Usually I'd stay up there until well past sunset, and I'd chain-smoke and gaze at the minuscule yards behind the buildings on Ninth Avenue and remember Etta and Tino and the splendor of Manhattan before it had changed me. Sometimes, when it was cloudy, I'd watch lights come on in the windows in the rear apartments in the buildings set on Ninth Avenue, as well as the people behind those windows as they did whatever they did.

At first I hardly noticed the people, just the lights, but as the days passed after the woman had been dragged, I cared less about the lights and more about what the people were doing. If they were in kitchens, I'd watch them prepare dinners and imagined the tastes of their meals; if they faced a TV, I'd wonder if they felt entertained, or where they worked, or if they had dates the next weekend. I felt unlike myself doing this, but it kept me from thinking about the woman who'd been dragged. Sometimes, as I watched, a bathroom window light would go on, and the first few times that happened, I looked back at the clouds for the stars. At some point, though, I glanced at what I could see in a bathroom, and there was something about people facing their mirrors while they groomed themselves, presumably to look good for others, that kept my eyes riveted.

While I'd watch them fix their hair or brush their teeth, I'd imagine their thoughts—as they stood behind a window between us, in a building I'd never been in—as if I were *them*. I sensed this meant I no longer wanted to live where I did, but I preferred to focus on their thoughts rather than mine.

Then 9/11 happened, and I know everyone in the city has a story about where they were when they learned the towers were hit, but I really don't care where you were when you learned— unless you or someone you knew were killed or hurt by those jets—because, relatively speaking, what does it matter? I mean, I know how claustrophobic it felt to live within walking distance of ground zero, because I went through that myself, but if everyone you knew survived 9/11 unharmed, you were lucky. Because the terrorists in those jets hated everyone in this country, and had they been able, they would have killed us all, but most of us survived. All I knew after 9/11 was that the sight of the woman being dragged felt connected to some universal hatred, and that I didn't know how to make that hatred disappear.

On the roof after 9/11, I was even more interested in what people in the buildings on Ninth Avenue were doing, if for no other reason than the lives of those people, like mine, had been spared. I didn't care, as I watched them, if they knew I saw them, to the point that one night, as a woman undressed in her bathroom, I didn't look away. I could see her naked back all the way down to her waist, and, when she faced me, I could see her breasts, and I was sure she saw me and that she knew I saw her, and that neither of us felt shame about what we were doing; we weren't hating each other, and that was good.

And after I returned to my apartment and locked myself inside, she was all that came to mind. Was she still in her bathroom? Why hadn't she bought curtains? Maybe, I thought, she prefers not to have curtains—maybe she, like me, feels claustrophobic. And I undid my locks and returned to the roof, where I saw that her bathroom light was off.

The window just to the right of her bathroom, though, was lit, its blinds raised halfway, and through the bottom half of that window, I could see her bed. She was stretched out on the bed, naked, possibly talking on the phone, and while I watched her, all sorts of thoughts ran through my mind, such as how you can be surrounded by millions of people who might want to help you but can't, or whether the woman who'd been dragged had been killed by a terrorist, which I knew wasn't likely but considered nonetheless. At some point I realized that, regardless of what had happened to the woman who'd been dragged, the sight of her had terrorized me more than anything ever had, more than my involvement in my mother's death, more than Carmen's tyranny over me, more than 9/11 itself, and when I returned to my apartment, it was far later than I'd thought, five minutes beyond the beginning of a Letterman re-run I'd never seen, meaning I'd killed more time than I'd thought possible.

I turned up the volume on the TV, and Letterman quipped about prostitutes in Times Square, and a camera aimed at the audience showed an old couple that was smiling without laughing, and when the camera zoomed in on the old woman, I realized that she was Etta. The show, I figured, could have been taped when I'd painted in Astoria without a television, and Etta could have been in the audience that night because she'd received two tickets in the mail, which could have happened because, sometime before the fire had blackened her apartment,

I'd mailed a postcard to the Ed Sullivan Theater asking that two tickets be sent to me care of her. She'd probably met the old man beside her after the last time I'd seen her, and I remembered her story about romance in the twilight of that old couple's lives. Then the camera shifted to the old man beside her, and he had the same peaceful smile as hers, but I couldn't stop picturing the sight of the woman being dragged—or feeling the hatred of people as far away as the other side of the world.

I clicked off the TV. As alive as I was, I felt worn. I pulled my blanket and pillow from the suitcase behind Ernest's wardrobe rack, turned off his overhead light, covered the couch, and tried to sleep. But I couldn't. I kept picturing the woman on the bed in the apartment on Ninth Avenue.

Then I heard footsteps in the corridor outside my door, which stirred memories of the evening the woman had been dragged. Headed toward me, the footsteps stopped just outside my door, and I wanted to turn on the light to make sure my locks were secured, but whoever was out there knocked.

I groped for my cell phone, hoping it was on the floor near the couch. But it wasn't. On the TV? I thought, and I crawled as quietly as I could over the bleached floorboards, then heard another knock. Someone, I thought, who knows the woman who was dragged. I found the light switch and turned on the light but couldn't see my cell phone anywhere.

Then I heard scratching on the other side of the door—someone trying to pick a lock? I was a foot from the door, the peephole daring me to look through it. The scratching stopped, then resumed. On tiptoes, I looked out the peephole and saw a face roughly twelve inches from mine, Ernest Coolridge's, his nose distorted by the curve of the glass, his eyes, from what I could tell, as steady as April rain, and even though I hoped he had news that would put my mind to rest about the woman who'd been dragged, I wished he would leave me alone.

Which he did. Which means what? I thought. And why did he stop by *now*?

Maybe, I thought, he just learned that the woman who'd been dragged was okay, and he wanted me to know as well. It's possible, I thought. And I somewhat

believed that. But only because, in Manhattan, everything always seemed possible. To prepare myself to live with suspicion of a death I might never know as
fact, I forced myself to glance at the floorboards, where that same death likely
occurred. Inches from the bottom of the door, I noticed a handwritten note on
familiar paper: a small, unlined sheet from Ernest's notepad, the result of the
scratching I'd heard. I picked it up, both halves of me—the hopeful one and the
one forced to doubt a woman's survival—prepared to conquer the other, but
the only belief I could count on just then was that the handwriting was indeed
Ernest's:

MICHELLE,

OUR DEAL IS
OVER.
MEET ME AT
LOEB BOATHOUSE
AT NOON. TO
DISCUSS
NEW WAYS TO
PAY RENT.

Chapter 23

I knew where the Loeb Boathouse stood—on the eastern shore of The Pond in Central Park—because, days after I'd moved in with Etta, I explored the park from Columbus Circle to the Met, though I'd never returned there because, on those seemingly meandering asphalt paths, I'd seen so many joggers wearing I ♥ NEW YORK shirts, it rubbed me the wrong way. I mean, I'd loved New York as much as anyone, but there was something about those shirts that bugged me: they seemed so bent on advertising the hearts of the throng that surrounded me, I wondered if, in fact, love in New York was impossible. All of those shirts reminded me of Thom's eight siblings, who, as children, had argued with each other only to run out of their house yelling "I love you" as they'd slammed their back door. To me, things like hearts and Valentine's Day and engagement rings work best if you just let yourself feel what they mean and never discuss them. You know: if love exists, it exists, and if it doesn't, it doesn't, and no amount of talking can change that.

Still, as I walked through mist toward the Loeb Boathouse to see Ernest, I couldn't help but think about love, because, of everyone I'd met in Manhattan, he'd been the person I'd loved most. Now that we were about to see each other for the first time since the woman had been dragged, though, I couldn't suppress the confusion I'd felt just before I'd received his note, inclusive as it was of hatred of him because he'd glanced in my direction just after I'd seen what I'd seen in the corridor. Hatred, I realized, was an extreme response to someone who might simply have appeared where he shouldn't have, but Ernest's involvement in whatever had happened to the woman who'd been dragged had shocked me into something far beyond disappointment. If he hadn't looked in my direction, I thought, would I feel attracted to Manhattan yet repulsed by the only apartment it afforded me? Would I be spending nights on a roof gazing at people I didn't know? Would I wonder, possibly forever, what happened to the woman who'd been dragged?

The closer I grew to the boathouse, the more I pictured Ernest's green comforter over those two helpless legs, and the less I could deny that, now that I was headed toward a new offer about how I could continue to live where I did, what had bothered me most about the woman who'd been dragged was that, when I calmed myself enough to hear my own heart, I was certain I knew who she was.

She, like me, had been a slave to Manhattan. Like me, she'd arrived there thinking she was someone secretly a cut above—a queen-princess-rock-star-model-diva-in-the-making—and that all she'd needed was to live in the world's hippest place to be developed or discovered. And she, like me, had known the odds weren't in her favor, but she'd believed in herself and leapt feet-first into the ridiculous prices, the talkers, the ass-grabbing, the bullshit of the hawkers on the sidewalk, the scams, the sight of black specks of soot on tissues when you blow your nose. And she'd been to clubs and met men who'd seemed kind, and she'd bought salads by the pound at rat-infested delis just after five PM to save a dollar a pound, and she'd tried to like sushi and suffered through food poisoning and the sharp smell of a grease fire in the apartment across the hall, as well as the darkness in her apartment during a six-hour brownout that never made the news, and, even indoors, she'd been stiffened by powerful noises that might have been gunshots or collapsed scaffolds or manhole covers shot up against the undersides of buses but could have been something else. And she'd lain awake wondering how she'd pay her phone bill. She'd watched her water run rusty. When the heat kicked on, she'd excused the clangs and hisses of the radiator because snow fell in such a torrent outside, she cherished warmth of any kind.

And there had been rats. And there had been mice. And she'd learned to smile at cockroaches. She'd thought about getting a cat but decided it wouldn't have been fair for it to spend a day as hungry as she'd been the time she'd eaten nothing but three carrots for thirty-seven hours straight not knowing whether she was trying to lose weight or save money.

And she'd crossed the paths of celebrities, actresses and disk jockeys and national news broadcasters and movie producers and athletes and rock musicians and rappers, and some of them had seen her, and, during the first month she'd lived there, exchanging glances with them had felt sophisticated, but she hadn't presumed her sophistication until she averted her eyes before celebrities noticed her. And she'd sung in her apartment and danced at clubs and danced at parties and after-parties. And it might not have felt completely right to walk into the after-hours club on the second floor of the cast-iron building in Tribeca, but once she'd been inside, some of the men were hip enough to avert their eyes until she danced onstage, when most of them smiled and talked to her as if they were her friends, which, the more she talked to them, the more they were.

And most of the other women at that club on the second floor of the cast-iron building in Tribeca were hip, too, arriving and leaving when they wanted, and, yes, there were jealousies among them, but far fewer than in an average sisterhood, and it *was* a sisterhood, maybe even a kind of family after a while, with a mother figure, Clarissa, who kept all of the women in line but just as well protected them: from the men; from the police; from the pettiness that finds affluent people who gather to eat, drink, and talk. Clarissa was the one who held fast to the rule that the club never was and never would be a strip joint. She insisted that when the women danced on stage, they did so only because the music was to their liking, and that if it weren't, no woman there needed to do anything on stage at all. And she made sure that if a woman wanted to dance on stage with another woman, she could, but that no woman ever had to dance with anyone, certainly not with the men who stood on the open dance floor between the bar and the stage itself. And she made sure all of the men spent money, on the unconscionable cover charge, on at least two drinks apiece, and on an entree of their choice, and that every woman there got a fair cut of every dollar that came in. Clarissa neither owned nor managed the place, but she kept the women who arrived happy enough to come back, and, without her, the place would have been just another after-hours club full of coked-up drunks looking for a piece of ass or an ear to fill with self-absorbed blather. She listened to the women there whenever *they* needed an ear, and she knew their names and where they were born and made their happiness necessary for hers. And if that place were owned by the mob, as rumor had it, she acted as the buffer to make sure none of the women there ever knew that as fact. She was a god, or a goddess, or a saint, or whatever you want to call it.

But Clarissa wasn't there the night Janet—the woman who'd been dragged—got the offer. Had Clarissa been there, Janet probably wouldn't have accepted the offer, or even known of it. The offer, I'll admit now, was that Janet be an escort in more of the common sense of the word—that is, not the kind of escort she'd been at the club. At the club, all Janet did was appear and dance with her clothes on and talk to whomever she wanted. Be a bitch if she wanted, be herself if it felt right. That's what brought Janet to the club, or at least what kept her coming back: she could be herself, no pressure, and make good money doing it, enough to pay rent and more. No sex, no lap dances, not even flirtation if she wouldn't have flirted otherwise. In other words, it all seemed so easy.

But the offer was one that asked her to depart from the understanding at the club. People at that club, especially the men, prided themselves in their agreement that the place wasn't a whorehouse or a strip joint or anything at all like either. It was a place they could be honest about with their wives; some of them even brought their wives, who, for the most part, seemed to enjoy its distinction. But the offer, for Janet at least, broke the rules. Not that anyone asked her to break any in-house rules. In fact, no one asked her even to bend the in-house rules that night, or on any night at all. The offer was for her to agree to a deal that would require that, during the day, usually during lunch hour, she'd make herself available away from the club, in Midtown, in an apartment where she and men could meet privately. She would never be obligated to do anything with a man who'd meet her in this apartment; if anyone made her feel uncomfortable, she could leave, no questions asked. She would merely be there, and could be herself there—she was encouraged to be herself there—and nothing had to happen except payment in cash to her of $500 an appearance, which would never require her to stay more than an hour. Payment would, according to the deal, be up front, to assure she'd need not make guarantees. They wanted company, these men, only the company of a woman they admired for her conversation, intelligence, and beauty. She could wear what she wanted, drink what she wanted—if she wanted. She could say what she felt, keep quiet if she so chose, disagree with the opinions of any man there. She'd be paid for her *presence*, which, according to the deal, was all these men sought from her.

If they wanted a streetwalker or a call girl, they'd look elsewhere. Just a friend, they told her. Just someone for them to be with to share a lunch hour after a morning in which they'd felt gutted by a firm that promised more wealth after they returned for another afternoon of work.

Of course, she probably sensed that, beneath all of this sophisticated innocence, there was always the possibility of a sexual advance. She was, after all, an attractive woman, the kind most men would die for, so if she'd decide she liked one of these men enough and find herself alone with him in this apartment, anything could happen.

So Janet had to know, when she agreed to this side-deal, that sex was always possible. I certainly knew it was possible after they'd offered this deal to me. And, yes, I'm admitting truths I haven't discussed since the woman was dragged: I was one of the women at that club in Tribeca who'd taken money to show up and look good. And I, like Janet, was also offered the side-deal to entertain men during daylit hours in an apartment in Midtown, and from moment one I felt the side-deal was shady, and that's why I declined it, but when Janet said yes to it, I never sat her down and told her that even though no one tried to pull anything on the women in that club, the side-deal—about lunch hours in the apartment—didn't sound right to me.

Worse, when Janet and I were standing side by side at the club and the side-deal was offered to us, I almost said it scared me but didn't want to sound like a hick, so I said, "I'm usually busy around noon," then glanced at Janet to shift the pressure of the offer on her, and she shrugged as if she weren't interested, then looked back at me, and I said, "What could it hurt?" Which was one of those things that, as you say it, you think, *Where is this coming from?*—and as she turned back to the two men who'd offered the side-deal and let them persuade her, I realized I'd endangered her because I'd been worried that she and the two men might think I thought too much, and I wanted to say something to take back those words—*What could it hurt?*—but I didn't.

But my steering of Janet toward danger wasn't the main reason I ignored the heart of the truth about her death until my second walk through Central Park. The main reason I ignored it for so long was that the apartment she died in was mine—and it had been up to me to decide whether to leave whenever she and a man stopped by.

Yes: what I'm saying is the side-deal Janet made with the two guys required her to meet men in the apartment where Ernest Coolidge was letting me live. And whenever Janet and a man stopped by, I would always leave. All I'd needed to do when they appeared that afternoon was say, "No, I'm not leaving; I have too much to do here." Or, even easier, just not buzz them in after they'd buzzed up and said they were downstairs. But I'd buzzed them in. I'd always buzzed

them in. And I'd always unlocked all of my locks and let them inside my apartment. And left immediately to allow a man to do what he wanted with her, for as
long as he wanted.

And the reason I allowed them stay longer than Ernest's rules provided was
because one of the men who brought her there paid me to. This man and I never
agreed out loud that he'd pay me, but when I'd come back and he and Janet
would be gone and I'd open the door to return inside, there would be three hundred dollars in an envelope placed behind the spigots of my little sink. Which
at first I'd thought was some kind of mistake. I'd thought maybe Janet or the
guy had forgotten to take it. So when they came by a week later, I asked them if
they'd forgotten anything the last time—"Like maybe an envelope?" I said—
and both of them looked me in the eye and shook their heads, and the man said I
should go out and treat myself to the kind of dinner I deserved. Which I took to
mean the money was meant for me, which I knew meant I was asking for something horrible to happen.

But I'd taken the money in those envelopes anyway. So now, as I grew closer
to the Loeb Boathouse, I hated myself at least as much as I hated Ernest. After
all, Janet could have been beside me right then, walking through the mist that
kept everyone but a few dog-walkers out of the park, if it hadn't been for *both*
Ernest and me. Half of me could blame Janet's death on him, but, if so, the other
half had to blame it on myself, and now all of me hated what we together had
done, and I still didn't know how to make hatred go away.

And you wouldn't feel like this, I thought as I walked on, if you hadn't left
Kankakee. I rounded a curve in the asphalt path and, through thickening mist,
saw Ernest Coolridge standing alone, facing the shoreline beside the boathouse,
that chunk of his jaw obviously missing even from my distance, and I couldn't
keep from thinking about how he looked as if he *were* Manhattan—old but still
alive, beleaguered but still proud.

"Ernest?" I called as I grew close.

He turned and faced me, sullen and drained.

"What's going on?" I asked.

He reached into his sports jacket for his notepad, removed a diminished pencil from behind his ear, jotted something, then tore off the sheet and handed it to me:

> HOW ARE
> YOU?

"Alive, Ernest. But that's not the question. The question is, what happened to Janet?"

He knotted his brow, a bluff so poor I was sure he felt as angry at me for asking as I was for needing to ask.

"You know who I'm talking about, Ernest," I said. "You saw me leave through the window at the end of the corridor. I mean, I don't see how you can expect me to live in that place now that I saw what I saw."

He nodded—barely—then sighed. He wrote:

> I DON'T.

"Don't *what?*"

> EXPECT
> YOU TO
> LIVE
> THERE.

"Then why did you ask me to come here?"

> I NEEDED
> TO KNOW

WHAT

YOU THINK
YOU SAW.

"I saw a woman being *dragged*."

Closing his bloodshot eyes, he raised a hand and nodded gently twice, telling me, I was sure, to compose myself.

"Well," I said. "What happened to her?"

He flipped to a new page in his notepad, readied his pencil, then froze. Then he wrote three words, underlining each one hard:

I
CAN'T
SAY.

"Why not?"

I DON'T
KNOW

PRECISELY
WHAT
OCCURRED.

I didn't believe him. But I couldn't raise my eyes from his notepad. Despite my certainty that, regardless of what I'd say, he'd never tell the truth, I said, "But you don't drag a woman—"

He placed his palm on my shoulder, shook his head, and folded his arms.

"She died, didn't she," I said.

He shrugged. Then he wrote holding his notepad close to his face. He studied what he'd written before he handed it to me.

> I KNOW
> WHERE
> SHE IS.

> LET'S
> LEAVE
> IT
> AT THAT.

"But Ernest—"

He raised a finger, his eyes on mine, stern and unwavering. Then he stepped beside me to let me watch as he wrote:

> YOUR
> KNOWLEDGE
> ABOUT HER

> COULD NEVER
> BRING HER
> BACK.

"But *you* know what happened to her."

He nodded.

"And?"

Again, I watched, and he scrawled:

> LET'S JUST

SAY

IT WASN'T
SOMETHING
I LIKE TO

THINK ABOUT.

Which confirmed at least one thing I'd feared: for all of his consideration, Ernest, like me, tried to keep the ugliest truths out of mind.

"You didn't go to the police, did you," I said.

He shook his head.

"Why not, Ernest? You should've gone to them. Why didn't you just go to them?"

Familiar noises, the kind that, in the past, had meant either impatience or anger, rose toward his jowls as he wrote.

I TOLD
YOU
WHY.

"When?"

IN ASTORIA.

"I'm not following, Ernest. So you're going to have to tell me again."

YOU'RE
LIKE
A DAUGHTER.

"So?"

> IF I
> TELL
> THE POLICE,

> YOU
> COULD
> DIE TOO.

And then I was sure everything was clear: Janet had been murdered, and I was in over my head, and Ernest was trying to protect me from whoever had killed her. His breaths grew louder as he wrote on, then rattled as they had when we'd stood on 49th Street watching Etta's building burn:

> PLEASE
> LEAVE
> THE
> CITY NOW.

"And go where?"

> I DON'T
> KNOW.

> IDAHO?

"It's Illinois, Ernest. And I hate it there."

> THEN TRY

IDAHO.
OR ANYPLACE

FAR.
(WHERE YOU'LL
NEVER SEE ME.)

Maybe, I thought, I'm putting *him* in danger. So I asked, "For your sake?"

FOR JANET'S.

SOMEONE
HAS TO

<u>LIVE</u>
FOR HER.

"And you can't?" I asked.

NOT
FOR

LONG.

"Because of your cancer?"

YES.

AND BECAUSE,

SOON—
WHEN MY
TIME IS UP—

I WILL TELL
THE POLICE .

Grinning, he flipped to a new page:

AT THAT
POINT,

WHO CARES?

"But Ernest. This is awful."

THAT'S WHY
YOU HAVE TO

GO.

"But how can I just...leave?"

HOW CAN
YOU NOT?

I frowned, then felt myself stiffen.

GO.

NOW.
IF NOT
FOR MY SAKE,
FOR JANET'S.

"Okay," I said.

And that was it. And then it seemed as if neither of us knew what to do. He did let me hug him, which I did as a daughter and an accomplice and a former enemy and a friend, and as I squeezed his dwindled shoulders, I heard a helicopter overhead, which likely meant some scared-to-death twenty-year-old was watching us to protect us from terrorists no one could see, and it struck me that, as much as Ernest looked like Manhattan, he also *felt* like Manhattan, because even though he'd endangered Janet and me, he had—since the first day I'd met him—done what he could to keep me alive. Thank him for that, I thought, but just after he released me, he mouthed the words *I know.* Then he slipped his notepad into the breast pocket of his sports jacket, lodged his little pencil behind his ear and kissed my forehead, and I tried to take his hand but managed only to touch his wrist, and he patted the backs of my knuckles to send me on my way, the hatred we'd faced thinning like the mist between us.

About the Author

Mark Wisniewski is the author of the novel *Confessions of a Polish Used Car Salesman*, the collection of short stories *All Weekend With the Lights On*, and the book of narrative poems *One of Us One Night*. His fiction has appeared in magazines such as *The Southern Review, Antioch Review, New England Review, Virginia Quarterly Review, The Yale Review, Boulevard, The Sun,* and *The Georgia Review,* and has been anthologized in *Pushcart Prize* and *Best American Short Stories*. His narrative poems have appeared in such venues as *Poetry International, Ecotone, New York Quarterly*, and *Poetry*. He's been awarded two University of California Regents' Fellowships in Fiction, an Isherwood Fellowship in Fiction, and first place in competitions for the Kay Cattarulla Award for Best Short Story, the Gival Press Short Story Award, and the Tobias Wolff Award.

Books from Gival Press - Fiction and Nonfiction

Boys, Lost & Found: Stories by Charles Casillo
ISBN: 978-1-928589-33-4, $20.00

Finalist for the 2007 *ForeWord Magazine*'s Book Award for Gay / Lesbian Fiction / Runner up for the 2006 DIY Book Festival Award for Compilations / Anthologies.
"…fascinating, often funny…a safari through the perils and joys of gay life."
—Edward Field

The Cannibal of Guadalajara by David Winner
ISBN: 978-1-928389-50-1, $20.00

Winner of the 2009 Gival Press Novel Award / Honorable Mention 2011 Beach Book Festival Award for Fiction / Finalist National Best Books 2010 Award for Fiction & Literature.
"…a devilishly delicious and disorienting novel. Food, sex, ghastly travel experiences, tantrums, *The Cannibal of Guadalajara* has it all, along with one of the most peculiar versions of the family triad in literary years."
—Joy Williams, a Pulitzer finalist, received the Strauss Living Award from the American Academy of Arts and Letters

A Change of Heart by David Garrett Izzo
ISBN: 978-1-928589-18-1, $20.00

A historical novel about Aldous Huxley and his circle
"astonishingly alive and accurate."
—Roger Lathbury, George Mason University

Dead Time / Tiempo muerto by Carlos Rubio
ISBN: 979-1-928589-17-4, $21.00

Winner of the 2003 Silver Award for Translation, *ForeWord Magazine*'s Book of the Year.
A bilingual (English / Spanish) novel that captures a tale of love and hate, passion and revenge.

Dreams and Other Ailments / Sueños y otros achaques by Teresa Bevin
ISBN: 978-1-92-8589-13-6, $21.00

Winner of the 2001 Bronze Award for Translation, *ForeWord Magazine*'s Book of the Year.
A bilingual (English / Spanish) account of the Latino experience in the USA, filled with humor and hope.

The Gay Herman Melville Reader edited by Ken Schellenberg
ISBN: 978-1-928589-19-8, $16.00

A superb selection of Melville's homoerotic work, with short commentary.

Gone by Sundown by Peter Leach
ISBN: 978-1-928589-61-7, $20.00

Winner of the 2010 Gival Press Novel Award.
"Almost no other novel treats the creation of sundown towns. *Gone by Sundown* thus amounts to a one-volume antidote to American amnesia. On top of that, it's a good read."
—James W. Loewen, author of *Lies My Teacher Told Me* and *Sundown Towns*

An Interdisciplinary Introduction to Women's Studies edited by Brianne Friel & Robert L. Giron
ISBN: 978-1-928589-29-7, $25.00

Winner of the 2005 DIY Book Festival Award for Compilations / Anthologies.
A succinct collection of articles for the college student on a variety of topics.

The Last Day of Paradise by Kiki Denis
ISBN: 978-1-928589-32-7, $20.00

Winner of the 2005 Gival Press Novel Award / Honorable Mention 2007 Hollywood Book Festival.
This debut novel "…is a slippery in-your-face accelerated rush of sex, hokum, and Greek family life."
—Richard Peabody, editor of *Mondo Barbie*

Literatures of the African Diaspora by Yemi D. Ogunyemi
ISBN: 978-1-928589-22-8, $20.00

An important study of the influences in literatures of the world.

Lockjaw: Collected Appalachian Stories by Holly Farris
ISBN: 978-1-928589-38-9, $20.00

Winner of the 2008 Appalachian Writers Association Book of the Year Award for Fiction / Finalist for the 2008 Golden Crown Literary Society Lesbian Short Story / Essay Collections Category / Finalist for the 2008 Eric Hoffler Award for Culture / Finalist for the 2007 Lambda Literary Award for Lesbian Debut Fiction.
"*Lockjaw* sings with all the power of Appalachian storytelling—inventive language, unforgettable voices, narratives that take surprise hairpin turns—without ever romanticizing the region or leaning on stereotypes. Refreshing and passionate, these are stories of unexpected gestures, some brutal, some full of grace, and almost all acts of secret love. A strong and moving collection!"
—Ann Pancake, author of *Given Ground*

Maximus in Catland by David Garrett Izzo
ISBN: 978-1-92-8589-34-1, $20.00

"...*Maximus in Catland* has all the necessary ingredients for a successful fairy tale: good and evil, unrequited love and loving loyalty, heroism and ancient wisdom...."
—Jenny Ivor, author of *Rambles*

Middlebrow Annoyances: American Drama in the 21st Century by Myles Weber
ISBN: 978-1-928589-20-4, $20.00

Current essays on the American theatre scene.

The Pleasuring of Men by Clifford H. Browder
ISBN: 978-1-928589-59-4, $20.00

"...deftly drawn with rich descriptions, a rhythmic balance of action, dialogue, and exposition, and a nicely understated plot. *The Pleasuring of Men* is both engaging and provocative." —Sean Moran

Second Acts by Tim W. Brown
ISBN: 978-1-928589-51-8, $20.00

2011 Runner Up for the New York Book Festival Award for Science Fiction / 2011 Winner of the London Book Festival Award for General Fiction.
"Really clicking, *Second Acts* is a picaresque, sci-fi / western, such as Verne or Welles might have penned it, but with tongue planted firmly in cheek. Tim W. Brown's tale of a husband's search for his fugitive wife takes readers on a whirlwind tour of America, circa 1830. In subverting history Brown's tale celebrates it, with a scholar's eye for authentic details and at a pacing so swift the pages give off a nice breeze."
—Peter Selgin, author of *Life Goes to the Movies*

Secret Memories / Recuerdos secretos by Carlos Rubio
ISBN: 978-1-928589-27-3, $21.00

Finalist for the 2005 *ForeWord Magazine*'s Book of the Year Award for Translations. This bilingual (English / Spanish) novel adeptly pulls the reader into the world of the narrator who is vulnerable.

Show Up, Look Good by Mark Wisniewski
ISBN: 978-1-928589-60-0, $20.00

Finalist for the 2009 Gival Press Novel Award.
"..a rollicking, laugh-out-loud romp of a novel, a picaresque spin through fin-de-siècle New York as seen through the eyes of its intrepid, Midwestern-born heroine...."—Ben Fountain, author of *Brief Encounters with Che Guevara*
"Wisniewski: a riotously original voice."—Jonathan Lethem

The Smoke Week: Sept. 11-21, 2001 by Ellis Avery
ISBN: 978-1-928589-24-2, $15.00

2004 *Writer's Notes Magazine* Book Award—Notable for Culture / Winner of the Ohionana Library Walter Rumsey Marvin Award. "Here is Witness. Here is Testimony."
—Maxine Hong Kingston, author of *The Fifth Book of Peace*

The Spanish Teacher by Barbara de la Cuesta
ISBN: 978-1-928589-37-2, $20.00

Winner of the 2006 Gival Press Novel Award / Finalist for the 2007 *ForeWord Magazine*'s Book of the Year / Award for Fiction-General / Honorable Mention for the 2007 London Book Festival.
"...De la Cuesta's novel maintains an accumulating power which holds onto a reader's attention not only through the forceful figure of Ordóñez, but by demonstrating acutely how ordinary lives are impacted by the underlying social and political landscape. Compelling reading."—Tom Tolnay, author of *Selling America* and *This is the Forest Primeval*

That Demon Life by Lowell Mick White
ISBN: 978-1-928589-47-1, $21.00

Winner of the 2008 Gival Press Novel Award / Finalist for the 2010 Texas Book Award for Fiction / Finalist for the 2009 National / Best Book Award for Fiction.
"*That Demon Life* is a hoot, a virtuoso tale by a master story teller."
—Larry Heinermann, author of *Paco's Story*, winner of the National Book Award

Tina Springs into Summer / Tina se lanza al verano by Teresa Bevin
ISBN: 978-1-928589-28-0, $21.00

2006 *Writer's Notes Magazine* Book Award—Notable for Young Adult Literature. A bilingual (English / Spanish) compelling story of a youngster from a multi-cultural urban setting and her urgency to fit in.

A Tomb on the Periphery by John Domini
ISBN: 978-1-928589-40-2, $20.00

Honorable Mention for the 2009 London Book Festival Award for Fiction / Finalist for the 2005 Gival Press Novel Award.
"Stolen antiquities, small-time thugs, a sultry femme fatale.... a book that takes the trappings of noir then transcends the genre...." *Bookslut*

Twelve Rivers of the Body by Elizabeth Oness
ISBN: 978-1-928589-44-0, $20.00

Winner of the 2007 Gival Press Novel Award
"*Twelve Rivers of the Body* lyrically evokes downtown Washington, DC in the 1980s, before the real estate boom, before gentrification, as the city limped from one crisis to another—crack addiction, AIDS, a crumbling infrastructure. This beautifully evoked novel traces Elena's imperfect struggle, like her adopted city's, to find wholeness and healing."
—Kim Roberts, author of *The Kimnama*

For a complete list of titles, visit: *www.givalpress.com*.
Books available via Ingram, the Internet, and other outlets.

Or Write:

Gival Press, LLC
PO Box 3812
Arlington, VA 22203
703.351.0079

Made in the USA
Lexington, KY
28 October 2011